"DEATH TO THE SCIENTISTS!"

The cry for blood vengeance went up all over the world. Too long had the people been ruled by the power of science. Now they would have their freedom, even if it meant plunging into a new age of barbarism . . . even if it meant destroying every man who threatened their ignorance with his knowledge.

John Wilson was a scientist, a great one. Only yesterday he had been famous, admired, secure. Now he was a hated enemy of society, a man on the run in a primitive, murderous world. And his brilliant intellect was at once his inescapable mark of fatal guilt, and his one slim, desperate chance for survival. . . .

THE
BURNING

JAMES E. GUNN

A DELL BOOK

Published by
Dell Publishing Co., Inc.
750 Third Avenue
New York, New York 10017

CONTENTS

PART ONE
WITCHES MUST BURN

I

The nightmare began when he was still five miles from the campus. For as long as he lived it would be *the nightmare* to him, never far from his unguarded moments. But then his life expectancy, at that moment, was not long.

The burning of the law building started it. The building was old and dry; it burned briskly, the flames leaping and dancing on the hill like malicious demons, spearing upward into the night, painting the other buildings with scarlet fingers.

There's been an accident, he thought, and poured kerosene to the old turbine under the hood. It responded nobly; the '79 Ford lunged forward.

An instant later he realized that the other buildings were burning, too; the scarlet fingers were their own.

When he reached the edge of town, the hill was a vast bonfire. The town sprawled under it, bathed in a sullen glare, dark-shadowed and lurid like a village in hell.

As he got closer to the campus, the streets became jammed with cars. He drove as far as he could, and then he got out and ran. Before he reached the top of the hill, some instinct of self-preservation made him strip off his tie and turn up his coat collar.

There were no fire trucks, no police cars. There was only the silent crowd, its dark face reddened occasionally by a leaping flame, its ranks impenetrable, its hydra-heads impassive. Only its eyes, holding within them their own small flames, seemed alive.

The law building was a crumbled ruin of stone and glowing coals. Beyond it was a tossing sea of fire, melting islands within it—the political science building, the library, the behavioral science building, the Union, the journalism school, the humanities tower, the auditorium. . . . For a moment he thought the administration building was untouched. But that was illusion; it was a shell—blank windows reddened by a dying glow.

It was summer, and the night was hot. The fiery death of what had been one of the Midwest's loveliest and finest universities made it hotter. But he was cold inside as he watched the labor and devotion of a hundred years burning, burning. . . .

A man ran toward the waiting crowd, a torch flaring in his hand, his face dark and unreadable, yelling, "Come on! They're running the eggheads now!"

For a moment longer the crowd waited and then, silently, it surged forward. For a few hundred yards he was carried with it, unable to fight free. At the brink of the hill, it dropped him. He stood there, unmoving, jostled by people who pushed past, not feeling them.

Beyond the hill were the physical science building, the experimental biology building, the building for business and economics. They were more isolated, more secure than those on top of the hill. Or so it may have seemed.

Now they, too, were burning. They were fire resistant and they burned less readily, but they burned. The flames roared in the night, and between the flames the forked, black figures ran back and forth. At every exit, the silent crowd waited for them with clubs and pitchforks and axes. Some of the black figures turned back into the flames.

The flames behind him and the flames in front, he watched, and all he could think about was that his papers were gone, charred and irretrievable, and the intolerable waste of five long years of labor and research. Even the Tool was gone.

Then, like a wave of nausea, the truth hit him. The black figures down there were people, people he knew and liked and respected, professors and their wives and their children. He turned aside and was sick.

As he straightened, he fought the impulse to run down the hill, to scream at the mob: "Stop it, you blind, killing fools! These are people, like you, living, working, loving, obeying the laws! You're killing yourself, the finest thing in you, and you're killing your country! Stop before it's too late!"

But it was already too late. Logic said it was futile. He would only die himself. He was important, not for himself but for what he knew and the promise that knowledge held.

Too many good men had died there already.

He closed his eyes and thought of Sylvia Robbins, who was intelligent, beautiful, as good a friend as any man ever had and might have been more if he had given it a chance, and who now lay dying down there. He thought of Dr. William Nugent, that tall, lean, iron-gray man of quick intuitions and relentless determination in his search for the truth. He thought of Dr. Aaron Friedman and Professor Samuel Black and a dozen others. . . .

And he thought: *If you are down there in that hell, my friends, forgive me. Forgive me, all of you, for being logical while you are dying. . . .*

And forgive them—the logicless, murderous mob.

He knew the people that formed this mob, their fears, their passions. He knew the savagery that moved them, the frustrations that demanded a scapegoat, the consciousness of guilt, of wrongdoing, of failure that cried out for an external soul to punish, that created one on demand.

They were unable to face the realization of "I was wrong—I made a mistake—Let's try a new line" that every scientist, every creative thinker must face daily. They needed the age-old, pain-killing drug of "He did it, the Other Guy—He's Evil—He made me Fail!"

And yet, knowing them so well, he did not know enough to stop them. He was five years, perhaps ten years away from the knowledge that he could take down the hill with him into their midst and find the right words and the right actions to make them stop—to turn them back into sane human beings.

The intuitive psychologists like the Senator were more capable than the scientists. But it is always easier to drive men insane than to lead them into sanity.

As he turned his face away from the scene of wanton murder and destruction, the knowledge that he was helpless was acid in his throat. A boy ran past, scarcely into high school, surely. He had a .22 rifle swinging in his hand. "Am I too late?" he shouted.

He didn't wait for an answer. Seeing the burning buildings and the black figures that ran between them, he swung his rifle to his shoulder and snapped off a shot. "Got one!" he exulted, his voice breaking with excitement. "Egghead!"

And John Wilson, egghead, slipped away. As soon as he had passed the fire's reflection, he hugged the shadows and made his way cautiously down the hill. He didn't go near his car. When he reached level ground, he walked briskly toward town.

Downtown was a half-dozen blocks of Massachusetts Street. It was deserted. Stores and restaurants and theaters were closed, their doors and windows protected behind metal gratings. The streets and sidewalks were cracked and rough; they hadn't been repaired for a long time.

Wilson reached the broad driveway of the bus depot. An old bus, its top battered, windows cracked, paint peeling, waited empty beside a side entrance.

The bus door was open; Wilson climbed aboard and slumped wearily into a back seat. Behind the driver's seat, the flat television screen was on. In the background was a picture of a university burning, Harvard or Cal Tech. As the camera shifted positions, Wilson saw that it was Harvard.

Senator Bartlett was superimposed on the flames. He was in his uniform, a worn, old, gray suit, a ragged blue shirt open at the throat. His unruly hair tumbled down over his forehead, and he brushed it back with a boyish gesture.

The burning university behind him gave him an aura of power to which he had only pretended until now. He seemed like an Old Testament prophet, as if he commanded the thunderbolt of the Lord and had directed it to strike here and there, to cleanse with fire the citadels of treason and immorality.

"My friends," said the Senator, sincerity ringing in his voice, the flames behind him like a halo, "news reaches us within the hour of another university in flames, and I say to you it is a regrettable thing. It is a tragedy. It is a fearful decision that has been forced upon this nation.

"But I say to you that they are not to blame who have thus taken justice into their own hands. They are not to blame who have carried destruction to the home of treason and brought death to traitors.

"They are to blame who have driven the people to this

desperate end. And they are paying the price for placing themselves above the people and above the welfare of their country.

"Know now and always that this is not my doing. My only suggestion was that local committees should be formed to decide what your children should be taught and to report any instances of Un-American teaching to my subcommittee on academic practices.

"But if traitors must die that their country live, then let them die. . . ."

Wilson stopped listening. He thought: *If they'd given us a few years more, a few months even. . . . We were on the right track at last; we could see light ahead. . . .*

His guess about the car had been accurate. There was a roadblock on the highway. All cars were being stopped; credit cards were being checked. In the bus, the vigilante group made only a visual check; no one thought an egghead would ride the bus.

A curious thing happened as the bus waited to get through. A blue ball of fire drifted down the highway, passing close to the self-appointed committee on credentials. It was closely followed by a red ball. At the roadblock men cringed in fear or fell to the ground or turned and ran.

Wilson knew what it was: St. Elmo's fire, a brush discharge of electricity, red when positive, blue when negative, most often seen at sea in stormy weather. Ball lightning.

Sometimes it was called *witch fire.*

At the bus depot in the city, Wilson picked out a phone booth behind a crackling neon sign, to foil the tappers, and, shielding the dial with his body, dialed quickly, nervously. At the other end the phone buzzed twice before it was lifted.

"Mark?" Wilson said quickly. "Is this Mark?"

There was a moment of silence through which came clearly the sound of someone breathing into the other mouthpiece. Then a woman's voice said: "John?"

"Is that you, Emily?" Wilson said. "What's the matter? Is Mark there?"

"Mark's gone—" she said flatly, "—on business. John —we didn't expect—we thought you would be—"

"No. It was almost over when I got there. I missed it."

"I'm glad," Emily said. "What do you want, John? I can't talk very long. I'm afraid this phone is tapped."

"Why should your phone be tapped?"

"We knew you." A pause. "Why did you call?"

"I need help, Emily. All I've got is the clothes I'm standing in. I thought you might be glad to hear I'm alive. I thought—you and Mark—" His voice trailed away into silence; the silence drew out painfully.

Emily took a breath; it rasped in the phone. "I'm sorry, John. We can't. You'll have to try somewhere else. We're in enough danger without running more risks. For all we know a neighbor or someone may have turned us in to the local Committee as intellectuals. We can't afford the disgrace or maybe worse. We've got to think of the children."

After a moment, Wilson said, "I see. You're thinking about the tappers. I'll come out."

"Don't do that!" Emily snapped. "Don't come near the house. They'll be after you now. We can't afford to be connected with you in any way. We aren't intellectuals! We graduated from college, but so did millions of other people. It's the scientists they're after and the teachers. Stay away from us, John!"

"I'm not hearing you right," Wilson said. "You and Mark—you're my best friends. It was just a few hours ago we were talking together, drinking together, laughing—"

"Forget that!" Emily said harshly. "Forget you ever knew us." She paused. "Try to understand us. You've got a plague, John, and it makes no difference how innocent or how right you are. You infect everyone you touch. If you were our friend, as you say, you would want to stay away from us."

"Is that Mark's attitude, too?"

"Yes."

"You mentioned your children," Wilson said softly. "You've got to think of them, you said. Think about them a little more; think about Amy and Mark, Jr. I'm not talking about the world they'll grow up to; you know what that will be as well as I. But when will you be able to look into their eyes, Emily? When will you be able to touch them without guilt, kiss them without feeling like Judas?"

"There are times when a person doesn't have a choice how he will live—it's be a coward and live or a hero and die. Women aren't heroes." There was another pause; Wilson was afraid she would hang up, but he couldn't think of anything to say. "Your best bet, John, is to head for the coast, either one," she continued finally. "I hear that some foreign governments are recruiting scientists and smuggling them out of the country."

"So that's the way it is?" Wilson said gently.

"That's the way it's got to be."

Wilson's voice turned as cold as hers. "I'll need money, Emily." With one hand he slipped his billfold out of his hip pocket, spread it open, and thumbed through the bills. There were only four: two tens, a five, and a one. "I'll need at least a thousand. I've got more than five thousand in the bank, but I can't touch it now. Send me the thousand and I'll mail you a blank check. You can cash it when things quiet down."

"No!" Emily said quickly. "Don't mail us anything. It might be intercepted or traced. We'll send you the money —call it a loan. How do you want it?"

"Cash," Wilson said grimly, feeling like a blackmailer, not caring. "Small bills. Send it to general delivery, down-town postoffice, addressed to me. My name's common enough, and they won't be hunting me so soon. Mail it tomorrow, Emily, as soon as the banks open. I can't stay here more than a day or two."

"All right, John." Emfly's voice was dry and distant. She had said her last word to him. No, there was one more. "Good-by."

Wilson hung up and leaned back wearily in the booth. He could try to reach Mark, but it would be difficult. Emily wouldn't let him talk to Mark at home, and the office was too dangerous. And he was half-certain that Mark was at home now, letting Emily cut him away.

Cross them off.

The depot was part of a block-long hotel. Wilson watched the depot and the hotel lobby for a few minutes. The parabolic mike on the wall was swinging hesitantly from conversation to conversation, but that was all right. You can't eavesdrop through glass; you have to bug or tap. No one seemed to be watching. But then he wasn't good at that sort of thing.

He dreaded leaving the booth, but it was a false security. He walked quickly to the hotel registration desk. "I'm —ah—nervous about fires," he said to the clerk. "Could you give me a room opening onto a fire escape."

The clerk looked at him curiously, but there was no help for that. "I guess so," he said. "Yes, here's one." He pushed a registration form toward Wilson.

Wilson picked up a pen and without perceptible hesitation wrote: "Gerald Perry." For hometown, he put: "Rochester, N.Y." For business: "Salesman." For firm: "G.E." For party affiliation: "Democrat." It was still safe enough to be a Democrat; the unaffiliated were the ones under suspicion, the independent voters who swung elections one way or the other. He didn't dare write: "Lowbrow." A precinct worker might visit him, or the clerk might ask for his party card.

"Salesman, eh?" the clerk said, studying the card. "How's business?"

"Lousy," Wilson said.

"That'll be six dollars."

"Sure," Wilson said. "Sure." He put down one of his ten-dollar bills.

The clerk gave him his change and rang for a bellboy. The bellboy was a spry, old man of about seventy. The clerk gave him the room key. "Good night, Mr. Perry."

This time Wilson's reaction was slow. He took a step away before he swung his head back and said, "Good night."

He got into the creaking, old elevator and turned around. A thin, dark-haired man was staring at something on the registration desk. As the elevator doors slid shut, he looked up. He stared straight at Wilson.

Wilson had never seen him before.

II

The hotel room was just big enough for a double bed, a ratty desk, an uncomfortable-looking overstuffed chair, a lamp, and a luggage rack. There was a tiny closet, a bathroom that was almost as small, and a window. The window opened onto a fire escape.

Wilson looked out. He was on the fifth floor. Rusty metal bars formed steps leading to a dark alley below.

He didn't look for bugs. They were there, no doubt, but he wasn't going to say anything.

He opened the window and sat down at the desk and emptied his pockets onto the ink-stained green blotter. The only incriminating items he could find were the cards in his billfold. There were dozens of them, including a handful of his own imprinted: John Wilson, Ph.D., Associate Professor, Department of Psychology. . . . There were cards from other professors and other schools. There were membership cards in professional societies, activity cards, library identification cards, and a host of others.

One by one, he burned them in the lavatory, crushed the ashes, and flushed them down the drain, saving only his driver's license and a couple of credit cards. He could find nothing else that would give him away as a teacher or an egghead.

Slowly, wearily, he stripped off his clothes and draped them over a hanger where the uneasy breeze would blow away the charred odor of smoke. He drew a hot bath in the cracked old tub and stepped in it, trying to keep his mind away from flames and screams and black figures running. Slowly his taut muscles relaxed. As they did, his tangled thoughts straightened out.

He could count on no help, none at all. If he were to get away, he would have to do it alone. That they would try to stop him, that they would be after him soon if they were not already, he had no doubt.

Somehow he should be able to make his knowledge and experience count. He had to. What were his resources? What was he?

He was a physicist specializing in electronics turned psychologist. His experimental work on the electroencephalograph had turned him toward what he had considered for so long a mere intuitive art, without measurements, without experimentally verifiable external data. Then he saw the opportunity for putting psychology on an objective basis.

With others, he had developed the Tool, the vital investigative device.

His thoughts came to a full stop. The Tool! That was

it. That was the edge he needed. It would take hard work and money to assemble a portable replica of the complex laboratory model in a few hours, but he could do it. The work he could handle, and unless Emily failed him he would have the money.

He was briefly glad that he had not drawn back from blackmail—which would not have been blackmail if Emily had been the friend she pretended to be. For Emily it would be conscience money and cheap at that. She had always felt that a financial contribution ended her moral obligation.

The bed's limed oak veneer was peeling. Wilson crawled gratefully between thin sheets and sought sleep. He would need his rest. But it was a long, long time before his mind would stop flipping up pictures before his reluctant eyes, and when he slept he dreamed of terror.

The door woke him with its thin, woody voice. "Mr. Perry," it whispered. "Mr. Perry!"

The window was still dark. Wilson looked at his watch. The luminescent dial indicated 4:32. Silently Wilson slipped out of bed and into his clothes.

"Mr. Perry," the door said urgently. "There is very little time. I must see you."

Wilson had no intention of seeing anyone at 4:30 in the morning, much less a door, much less a door that called him by a name he had used only once. He knew how it was done, of course: some resonating device for foiling the bugs. Or for tricking him into thinking that was what it was for.

He slid out the window and made his way silently down the fire escape, keeping close to the wall in the dark. The last flight of steps screeched as his weight overbalanced it toward the ground. Then he was in the alley. The stairs swung back up noisily. He crouched there, waiting for discovery, but there was no more sound.

A stray beam from the nearby street swirled toward him. The night was filled with smog, strong in his nose, acrid in his throat. Ninth Street was deserted.

Where could he go at 4:30 in the morning?

He started walking south, briskly, working the stiffness out of his legs and the sleep out of his mind. The vital thing was to get out of the area immediately.

An all-night restaurant was open on Twelfth. It was little more than a diner; stools lined a single counter. A sleepy-eyed short-order cook was alone in the place. Disinterestedly, he watched Wilson take a stool and study the menu. Wilson punched his selection.

The cook took a toothpick out of his mouth and said: "It's broke. Some guy yanked out a handful of wires the other day."

"Yeah?" Wilson said. He was careful not to speak precisely. "I'll have ham 'n' eggs, hotcakes, an' coffee."

"Okay." The cook poured batter out of a metal pitcher onto a black griddle, took a small, thin slice of ham out of the refrigerator and slapped it down beside the pancakes, and with bored skill cracked two eggs one-handed into a skillet.

"Whatsa matter with the gadget?" Wilson asked, nodding at the automatic, high-frequency cooker.

"These fancy machines are always getting out of whack. Besides, they just throw people outa jobs, right? What good is that?"

"Yeah," Wilson said.

"You hear about the big fire?"

"Yeah."

"About time somebody showed those eggheads who's runnin' things," the cook growled. "They're like the cooker—fancy and complicated and always breaking down. Inventing things, throwing people outa work, starting wars, betraying our secrets to anybody that wants 'em. They're no good, and it's time they got wise. The Senator'll show 'em."

It was, most certainly, time they got wise. Wilson didn't bother pointing out the inconsistencies in the man's argument. He was thinking about Sylvia and Bill Nugent and Aaron Friedman and Sammy Black. "Yeah," he said.

Wilson lingered over breakfast for an hour, sipping four or five cups of coffee, keeping a wary eye on the front window, but finally he had to leave. The cook was looking at him too often.

He thought of the library and discarded the idea immediately. It was too characteristic, and the local committee might well have spy-eyes on it for permanent surveillance.

Instead, he walked the streets. Now he was not alone. The sun had come up, and the smog had started to thin. People were hurrying to their jobs; buses rolled noisily along the streets, disgorging their cargoes.

He looked up once to find himself passing the library. *So much,* he thought grimly, *for the subconscious.* The windows and doors were boarded up. The building had died long ago.

He passed the postoffice and looked at it longingly, but it was too early.

At the corner a newsstand was yelling headlines: "UNIVERSITY BURNS! HUNDREDS DIE IN BLAZE! ARSON SUSPECTED!"

He put a quarter into the machine and took the paper into a self-service drug store. He bought a Coke from a dispenser and took it to an empty booth. He spread the paper out on the table.

The front page was devoted to pictures and stories about the fire. One section of a story caught his eye. It said:

> Although no witnesses to the start of the holocaust have been identified, local police have denied the rumor that it was set by an incensed mob of townspeople later swollen by additions from surrounding towns and cities.
>
> There is evidence that the blaze was touched off by university teachers themselves in an attempt at martyrdom to gain sympathy for the egghead cause, asserted a police spokesman, who refused to be quoted directly.
>
> A plot has been uncovered to discredit the Lowbrow movement and the Senate Subcommittee on Academic Practices, this spokesman stated. But the flames spread beyond control, and many of the arsonists and their families were burned alive.
>
> Area law enforcement officers have been alerted to be on the lookout for university employees who may have escaped the general destruction, and a broadspread appeal has been made to the public to report anyone whose actions or speech is suspicious.
>
> The ashes of the gigantic fire are still being combed for bodies and identification compared with the university roster.

As yet there was no list of the dead and missing. In a black-bordered box was a brief item with a Washington dateline:

Senator Bartlett announced early today that investigators from his staff would aid the authorities in their search for the arsonists. The guilty eggheads, he said, should be charged with arson, murder, and treason and the maximum penalty assessed—if they are brought in alive.

Wilson stared blindly into a corner of the booth. So, he thought, there was an open incitement to murder. The eggheads were guilty before the investigation began, in spite of such inescapable evidence as wounds and broken bones and Senator Bartlett's own statements on the broadcast of the night before.

But this was a world eaten with a terrible cancer of suspicion and fear. It was a world in which truth was only a weapon to use against your enemies and your neighbors, if you could twist it into the right shape.

It was not exactly a world in which black was white and white was black; it was a world in which no color existed independently of the viewer. There was no objective reality to agree upon.

It was his world, and there was nothing he could do about it but run.

He was a seedy, middle-aged down-and-outer with a gray stubble of beard on his seamed face. Wilson didn't look much better; he hadn't shaved, and he had rumpled his clothes artfully. Wilson tried to get through to the d-and-o with his instructions, but the man just nodded his head vaguely.

There was no help for it. Unless there was trouble, the d-and-o could do the job as well as anyone; if the man was picked up, that was the end of it, and at least he couldn't identify Wilson.

"They'll want identification," Wilson said. "Here's a credit card, and here's the five bucks. Got it straight now?"

"Sure, sure," said the d-and-o. "I go up to the general delivery window and I—"

"Okay," Wilson said. "Get going!"

"Can't I have a drink now?" the man whined. "Ain't had a drink yet this morning, and I'm dry." His hand rasped across his mouth. "Lost my job to a gold-durned machine, I did. Damned eggheads did it. Haven't had a job since."

"Afterwards," Wilson said inflexibly.

"Okay, mister," the man said. "It's your money." He folded the bill and stuffed it into the pocket of his dirty pants.

Wilson gave him half a block, watching him through the fly-specked saloon window, and then started after him.

Moving slowly, the d-and-o climbed the broad, post-office steps and disappeared into the dimness under the tall columns. Wilson hurried to keep him in sight.

He felt a moment of panic as he couldn't find his messenger inside, and then he spotted him to the right, up a short flight of stairs. Wilson faded back toward the wall.

The d-and-o ambled up to the broad window marked: GENERAL DELIVERY. He said something to the clerk and showed the credit card. A moment later he collected a small package wrapped in brown paper.

Slowly, while Wilson held his breath, the man turned south toward the side entrance. After a moment, Wilson followed. So did two other men, detaching themselves from a writing desk near the general delivery window.

As he passed through the exit, the d-and-o bent and straightened. Wilson's eyes were on his hands. They were empty.

At the door, Wilson looked down. The package was almost invisible behind a scraggly bush. Wilson stooped smoothly and had it and walked on.

He glanced back over his shoulder. The other two pursuers had caught up with the d-and-o; they grabbed him by the shoulder roughly and spread out his hands. As Wilson walked quickly in the opposite direction, he had a twinge of conscience. He smothered it quickly. They would soon discover their mistake and let the man go, and the d-and-o would consider it cheap if they held him overnight.

He had been betrayed, Wilson knew, and there was no doubt in his mind who had done it. Emily had turned him in, virtuously, with a firm belief that she was sacrificing something precious to save her family, as a mother in other times would have sold her virtue to buy food.

Wilson shrugged. The risk had been necessary. The only thing that bothered him now was whether the package was filled with money or cut paper.

He opened it in the privacy of a barber shop men's room. There was money in it.

He smiled ironically as he stowed the thick bundle of bills away in his billfold and inside coat pocket. It was as natural for Emily to pay for a bit more protection as it was for him to suspend final judgment until all sides of a question were investigated.

Either way it worked out, Emily was safe.

There are that kind of people in the world. They are the kind who survive.

Wilson bought himself fifteen minutes in a shower stall and a cellophane-wrapped package of new underclothes. The shower sprays didn't work well, and the underclothes were too big, but he enjoyed them both. He skipped the shave. His face and his suit had reached the proper state of unkemptness.

He got a quick lunch at a stand-up cafeteria. When he finished he walked along the sidewalk reading window signs until he found one he liked. It said: HEARING AIDS.

He pushed his way into the store past a stubborn automatic door that refused to be automatic. At the rear, an old man looked up from a desk littered with electronic parts and moved to the counter. The flesh-colored, almost invisible cord of a hearing aid was taped to his neck. "I told you," he said in a tense, high-pitched voice, "I don't want no protection—"

"I don't know what you're talking about," Wilson said. "I want a hearing aid, an all-transistor model."

"Mistook you for someone else," the old man said grumpily. "One of these Committee hoodlums trying to get me to contribute. Calls it 'riot insurance.' Broke my door the other day. You don't look hard of hearing."

"It's not for myself; I'm getting it as a present."

"Should have the person come in for tests himself, by rights. Makes a difference what kind of aid you need."

"I know, but I want to get one now. He can get it tested later, exchange it if he has to."

"Poor way to do things." He studied Wilson with faded blue eyes. "Well, how much you want to pay? We got 'em in all price ranges."

"Your best."

The old man nodded with just a trace of friendliness

now and shuffled toward the rear of the store. He came back with a small box in his hand.

Wilson said: "How's business?"

The old man shook his head. "No good. People got a notion nowadays that there's something wrong with new-fangled gadgets, that people should stay as God made them. Silly, damn fools. God made them stupid, too, but they don't have to stay that way unless they want."

He slapped the box down on the counter and opened it up. He explained the workings of the hearing aid for fifteen minutes before Wilson could get a word in.

"How much?" Wilson said finally.

"How's that?" said the old man, slipping his hand under his linen jacket to adjust the volume control.

"How much is it?" Wilson said loudly.

"Don't have to shout. That'll be $239.95." He looked wistfully at the box. "They don't make 'em like that anymore. That's all right, though. They don't buy 'em anymore, either."

Wordlessly, Wilson counted out the money.

Directly across the street was an electronic parts store. It was a big place with a counter stretching across the front and all the way down one side. There was no one in the store except a clerk. He looked up, surprised, as Wilson entered, and hurried to the front.

"You've got a workroom, haven't you?" Wilson said without preliminary.

"Sure," the clerk said, nodding his head at the partition behind him. "Best in town."

"I want to do some assembling. I'd like to rent the room and the use of your tools for the rest of the afternoon. I'll pay for whatever parts I use and twenty bucks more."

"Okay," said the clerk, his eyes wide. "And if you need any help, just whistle. I haven't had a customer in days."

Five hours later Wilson dropped the tiny soldering iron, took the jeweler's magnifying glass out of his eye, and rubbed his eyes wearily. On the bench in front of him was the hearing aid, but the old man across the street would never have recognized it. It was completely re-wired and connected to another flat box about the same size. That box, in turn, was connected to a fanlike antenna of fine wire sewn into his coat between the lining and the coat itself.

The original hearing aid went into his right-hand jacket pocket, the new one into his left-hand pocket. Wilson pressed the tiny bone-conduction speaker to the mastoid behind his left ear, turned on the power, and hoped for the best. He had not tried for too much, and he had not gotten much. That little he needed.

It was almost six in the evening when he walked out of the workroom and reached the customer side of the counter. The clerk was idly flipping the pages of a tattered parts catalogue. He looked up. The speaker buzzed.

Curiosity, Wilson translated. "That's one hundred fifty-three bucks, right?"

"Right," said the clerk. "Say, I don't know what your business is—I don't want to know—but there's a thin, dark haired guy across the street watching this place. He's been there all afternoon."

Wilson looked through the front window. It was him, all right, the man from the hotel. "Got a back door?"

"Through there. Opens into the alley."

"Thanks. Here's another ten. Forget you ever saw me."

III

The chair car was peeling chromium and worn upholstery. Wilson sat wearily in his upright chair—the tilt-back didn't work—and stared out his window into the night. The metal wheels clacked as the train picked up speed getting out of the city, and the car swayed gently.

Wilson's eyelids drifted down, and he propped them open again. It had been a long day and an exhausting day, but he couldn't let go. Not yet.

He was on his way. Not to either coast, as Emily had suggested. That was what they'd expect. He was enroute to a port city just as convenient as New York or Los Angeles or San Francisco, and it was closer and less obvious. He was on his way to New Orleans.

If he had to leave the North American continent, as he did, he preferred South America over the other possibilities. There had been hints in professional magazines.

Now he put them together. Recruiting had been parceled out geographically. The African republics were hiring at New York, and the west coast ports were being used by Australia, the Chinese empire, and the splintered Indian states.

But the best facilities for psychological research were in Brazil and Venezuela; they had some excellent psychologists and sociologists of their own. He had met a number of them at a Pan-American Conference in Caracas before it became impossible to get a passport for any kind of conference and asking for one was asking for trouble.

Perhaps Brazil would be the best choice. It was in the middle of a massive economic assault on its unexploited resources. The economy was expanding faster than the stock exchange could keep up with it. Research grants would be easy to get, and the grantors would be too busy to pry into what he was doing. . . .

The earphone buzzed softly. "Tickets?" said the conductor.

Wilson straightened up. "I'd like to turn in my chair car ticket for a bedroom or a compartment. I didn't have time to make a reservation."

The conductor's theta rhythms didn't speed up as he made a pretense of checking his reservation cards. "Well, now, I think we can take care of you. We have a bedroom in Car 110 just ahead. Bedroom C. What's the name?"

"Lester Craddock," Wilson said promptly, "with two *d*'s and a *ck*. Thanks, conductor."

"That's all right," he said, his red face pleasant. "Things are a little loose on Wednesdays anyhow."

Within ten minutes Wilson was between cool, nylon sheets. Like himself, they were a little frazzled around the edges, but they were still serviceable.

He let the train's gentle motion rock him to sleep. The nightmare didn't return for a long time.

He woke and the rocking and the clack-clack of the wheels were unchanged, but the sunlight was streaming in around the edge of the curtain and through one long, patched tear across it. He looked at his watch: 8 o'clock. He had slept for almost ten hours. He could stop running now and start thinking.

Yesterday, unaware, he had been on the ragged edge of

nervous exhaustion. He had blundered ahead haphazardly, riskily. It was a wonder he had not been caught. He had gotten the money and fixed the Tool, true, but there had been simpler and safer ways to do it. He had been on the verge of hysteria.

Now it was different. He was out of the deadly area unsuspected. He had an aid no one would suspect; not the equal of the room-sized laboratory model, which could almost talk, but the simple analysis of theta brain rhythms gave him a vital warning system, a kind of basic lie detector. And he was on his way.

He got up and washed. He shaved with the electric razor he had bought at the station and brushed his teeth with the railroad's toothbrush. He dressed, slipping into the jacket with the heavy pockets, and pressed the speaker button behind his ear. It hummed softly, picking up a reflection of his own brain activity.

Wilson walked down the swaying aisles, listening to the rise and fall in pitch and intensity of the earphone as the theta rhythms changed, watching the faces of the people he passed. No one seemed unduly excited as they looked at him.

When he got back from a leisurely breakfast in the dining car, the room was made up. He settled himself in the chair by the window and stared out at the flat river-bottom land fleeing past him toward the north.

The earth was summer-green and lovely with the sun laying across it. A distant jet liner drew pencil-thin, white vapor trails across the sky. On the glistening ribbon of the tollway looping the hills beside the tracks, a gleaming, new Cadillac Turbojet 500 kept pace with the train for a few miles. Its top was retracted; a girl was driving, and the wind blew out her long, blond hair, pulling back her head like an anxious lover. And then she raised one white arm in a carefree wave and poured kerosene to the turbine and outdistanced the train within a few seconds.

No one would have suspected, sitting here, looking out upon the fertile land and man's conquest of it, that a blight lay upon the earth, that the world man knew was dying of it. It was not nature that would conquer man; man would conquer himself. He was the only one who could do it.

The blight was anti-science. It seemed like a natural, human thing to be against this neurotic necessity for eternal progress, to long for the simpler, saner life, but it was a basic self-negation of everything that made man human. It attacked the innermost core of man's distinction from the blind forces of the universe, and it would level man back into his old equality with the animals and the vegetation. They didn't adapt their environments; they adapted. That was their method of survival.

Science was not a laboratory or a technology or a gadget; science was a way of life. With their minds, it said, men can understand the universe, and understanding will make it a comfortable, human thing. There were no dark, unfathomable mysteries, no secrets men should not know, no knowledge forbidden.

Deny that, and you opened the door to darkness and despair, to old superstitions and new fears; you made man a slave again. He had been master now for long generations. He had made earth his, and the space around the earth, and he was reaching out toward the other worlds of the solar system. But now, through some, strange, suicidal psychosis, man was turning upon the quality that set him apart; he was destroying himself.

A wise man could have seen it coming a long time before, could have prepared for it, perhaps, could have fought it. But there was no one wise enough—or even if there was, he could not make himself heard, he could not rally support, he was a voice crying in the wilderness.

It had been hard to recognize. Anti-science was a continuous thread through the fabric of man's intellectual history, an antithesis to the thesis of man's conquest of his environment, winning sometimes, losing sometimes, but mostly developing out of the conflict a new synthesis.

So it would have taken a very wise man to have seen that the growing anti-scientism of the seventies was different in kind than the absolute anti-scientism of the medieval church, say. But the twentieth century had seen science altering man's environment in a geometric progression, increasing his command of earth's resources, making earth a fairer, more comfortable place in which to live. In this context anti-scientism was an ugly revulsion, not a turning away to another frame of reference.

It had not taken the catalyst of war to precipitate incipient distrust into active rebellion. The slow grinding of two great world powers against each other had nurtured it, had held it in, and Senator Bartlett had come out of nowhere to give it vent.

Harvard in the east had been the first to go, then Cal Tech in the west, and then—Wilson shuddered, remembering.

Houses flashed past the window. The train slowed as it entered a city. In the corridor outside, the conductor called, "Alexandria!" A few minutes later, the train crept up to a station and stopped.

At the university, they had been close to what looked like a solution. If man exhibits symptoms of homicidal insanity, then, truly, the only proper study of mankind is man. If society makes pariahs of those members who have contributed most to what it is, then those members should study society. What was needed was a science of man, call it anthropology, psychology, mass psychology, sociology, political science, or what you will. And quickly —before *scientist* became a deadly word.

The electroencephalograph, developed and improved, had become their Tool—Sammy Black had called it that and Tool it had been—for supplying external evidence of what goes on inside the head. They had identified and analyzed alpha rhythms, theta rhythms, and delta rhythms, matched them with actions, reactions, stimuli of all kinds —including words.

Words were one of the keys. It is in words that we think, and it is in words that we do most of our communication. Through words we learn about the world, and through words society teaches us its social and cultural patterns. All this makes its impression on language, and in it can be read the structure of society. Words take on emotional and action content; learn to manipulate them properly and you can make people do whatever you wish.

Demagogues had learned that a long time ago. Advertisers had learned it more recently. But they were intuitive artists, and art cannot be taught.

So at the University they had been compiling a Dictionary, the first real dictionary the world had ever had. Later would come an analysis of the structure of language and perhaps the development of the Tool into a true psionic device which would pick up and transmit thoughts themselves.

Now all that was lost, the Dictionary ashes, the Tool twisted, indecipherable metal. Granted the time and the money, it would take him years to get back to where they had been. And he was afraid he didn't have years.

It was symptomatic of the scientist's blindness to social values and social dangers that it had taken the shock of a university's murder to make him realize that the Tool was more than a research device; it was a weapon, warning against surprise, a clue to the intentions of his fellow men. As he sat there, thinking, the phone began to buzz. The note climbed slowly in pitch and intensity until it reached a shrillness that brought him to his feet.

The door rattled as someone took hold of the handle. Slowly it swung inward. He had forgotten to lock it!

In the doorway, his theta rhythms expressing a violent excitement was the thin, dark-haired man Wilson had seen twice before.

"Dr. Wilson?" he began.

Wilson's fist was already swinging. It caught the man squarely on the jaw. He collapsed slowly, turning a little, his eyes glazing.

Anyone who had followed him this far and knew his name knew too much.

Wilson caught him before he hit the floor, kicked the door shut with his heel, and stowed the man on the broad seat, his face to the cushion. Only then did he notice that the window shade was three-quarters of the way up. Anyone watching on the platform could have spotted him.

There was no one on the platform now. Wilson pulled down the shade, got his little handbag of possessions, picked up a cardboard sign, and walked out of the compartment. He hung the sign on the outside of the door: DO NOT DISTURB.

He strolled down the aisle and out onto the platform. He watched the train pull away.

IV

The used car gave up thirty miles out of Alexandria. The intense turbine temperature melted a concealed crack that had been patched with solder. It blew out with finality. The car had been a gamble that hadn't come through.

Wilson knew the car had been wrecked. That was the only reason he could pick it up for less than two hundred dollars. But he had hoped that the turbine was as sound as it seemed.

Thoughtfully Wilson crawled out from under the hood just as a sun-yellow Cadillac slid to a stop beside him, its brakes screaming in pain. He had seen the driver before. Her hair matched the car, and she had driven along beside the train that morning.

"Turbine gone?" she called cheerfully.

"Utterly," Wilson said.

"What are you going to do?"

Wilson shrugged. "Walk, I guess, unless some kind driver takes pity on me."

"Don't look at me with those big, brown eyes, guy," she said. "I got a heart like a ripe cantaloupe. Where you going?"

Wilson cast away caution. "New Orleans."

The Cadillac door nearest him slid open. "Hop in. That's where I'm going."

Wilson got in. The door slid shut behind him. Immediately the car began to accelerate quietly, swiftly. Within seconds they were rolling along the tollway at 100 miles per hour.

"Do you do this often?" Wilson asked dryly. "Pick up strangers, I mean?"

She gave him a swift, sidelong glance. "Sometimes. When they have big, brown eyes."

"Then you've lived a fine, full life, and I'm surprised it's lasted so long."

"So am I," she said softly. "But then the world is going to hell in a worn-out hack, and who cares?"

The wind had her hair and streamed it out behind, a bright, golden scarf tugging at her head. Her blue eyes were young and alive; her lips looked soft and warm; her throat was a smooth, white column.

She was no older than 25 or 26. A child. Her fingers were bare.

Wilson frowned and looked at the unwinding ribbon of tollway. He had thought all that was finished with Sylvia, but life went on, uncaring.

There was always something just a little phony about

blondes, he thought, even the real ones: a reputation, perhaps, that they had to live up to. But there was nothing phony about this one.

Maybe he was just susceptible.

The girl's theta rhythms were swift, and the speaker buzzed in his ear. But there was little oscillation; she just lived faster.

"I've never been in a Cadillac before," he said.

"Poor man?"

"I guess. I never thought about it."

"Good. Nothing different about a Cadillac—got a turbine and four wheels just like a Ford. Fancier is all."

"I've heard they'll go two hundred," Wilson said.

Laughter crinkled her eyes as she glanced at him. "I've had this to two fifty myself. Watch!" She pushed on the accelerator. The car leaped forward. Wind resistance lifted the nose until the rocketlike hood ornament was pointed above the horizon and the car seemed about to take off. The tires whined on the cracked, worn pavement.

The speedometer needle moved swiftly past 150—175—200. At 225, it began to slow. It came to a stop a little past 250.

Wilson tore his eyes away from the broad, pockmarked ribbon of concrete leaping toward him and diving under the car, and he looked at the girl. She was staring straight ahead, her lips parted, her theta rhythms elated.

Over the noise of the wheels, Wilson shouted: "Aren't you afraid the tires will blow?"

"Why?" she shouted.

He shrugged.

"Bother you?" she asked.

She swung out to pass a truck, and Wilson's eyes swiveled involuntarily back to the road. The car rocked perilously on two wheels before it decided to settle back.

"I'm not in this much of a hurry," he said calmly.

"Okay," she shouted and let up on the accelerator. When the needle had dropped back to 100, she said, "You're all right. When the speedometer reaches two hundred, lots of men reach for the wheel, and when it passes two fifty, pass out."

"I know why it doesn't worry you to pick up strange men off the tollway," he said grimly. "If they get dangerous you can scare them to death."

She laughed gleefully and looked very young. "My

name's Pat Helman. I'm old Mark Helman's only child, and I have a guilt complex a runway long."

"What have you got to feel guilty about?"

"About being the daughter of a man who cared more about building rocketports and artificial satellites than building a sound society, who put more into the conquest of space than into the conquest of himself. Sometimes, in this car, I can almost outrun my guilt, and then I feel guilty about being a girl who tries to escape from problems instead of staying to solve them."

"Well, then," Wilson said with a brief smile, "hello, Pat Helman." He took a chance. "My name is John Wilson."

"I know," she said. "My job was to watch for you along the tollway."

The sun-yellow Cadillac hurtled southeast along the old tollway toward New Orleans, and Wilson sat back, wordless. Finally he said, "Was it smart to tell me?"

She smiled. "I didn't say I was smart."

"What's to stop me from knocking you out and taking over the car?"

"At one hundred or"—her foot pushed against the accelerator—"one fifty? A Lowbrow might, but you're a sensible man, Dr. Wilson. You know we'd both be killed if you tried that. And that wouldn't be sensible."

"You give me too much credit," Wilson said gloomily.

"But if you were a Lowbrow I'd tell you I had the evil eye." She twisted one blue eye into a malicious squint. "Behave or I'll strike you dead. Actually there's a hypodermic under the seat loaded with ten cubic centimeters of a fast-acting anesthetic. If I touch the horn, you'll get a shot that will put you out for three to four hours. I don't want to do that, Dr. Wilson."

He moved uneasily on the yellow-plastic seat. "Why not?"

"I like you; I want to help you."

"Help me into the hands of Senator Bartlett?"

"No."

"Who are you working for? The local police? The F.B.I.?"

"No. And I can't tell you who I am working for or what they want with you. I'm just an errand-girl, and I don't know enough. Even if I did, I might say the wrong thing. My job is to deliver you to the people who can tell you."

"And because you've been honest twice I'm supposed to trust you this time."

She shook her head. "You're supposed to come along because you must—because we're both in the same car and you can't get out."

"I don't trust you," Wilson growled. "No one who uses force can be trusted."

"Sometimes force is necessary. When a child is about to walk off a cliff or a homicidal maniac gets his hands on a loaded gun, there's no time to argue."

"I'm neither one nor the other," Wilson said stiffly.

The tires sang to them, and the tollway spun away beneath the tires. Pat glanced at Wilson sideways and said: "This is the world, isn't it? A high-powered car rocketing down the tollway carrying its human passengers willy-nilly toward an unknown destination. The car is human civilization, and I'm the driver. I built it, too, me the scientist, the engineer. I kept streamlining the car and souping up the horsepower; I didn't know where the car was going either, but I wanted to get there in a hurry. Destinations weren't my job. My job was to build a faster car."

"That's right," Wilson said firmly. "It isn't the scientist's job. His job is to find the facts and seek the truth. He can't concern himself with goals because his only reality is what he can locate and what he can measure. Goals can't be measured; they're problems for philosophers."

"And if there are no philosophers or the philosophers are wrong and you know they are wrong, what then, scientist? But you aren't the scientist now. You're the mass of humanity being hurtled along in a juggernaut you don't understand toward a destination you can't imagine. The driver knows the car is going in the wrong direction, too—just as you know, John Wilson, that New Orleans is the wrong direction for you—but, you see, he isn't really driving. The steering wheel doesn't work.

"The passenger doesn't know that, but he knows that the driver is lost, too. You are the passenger. You were fascinated by sheer speed, for a while, but at last you know that something is wrong.

"You react blindly to stop the car in the only way you know. You reach over and grab the driver by the throat and start choking him. You've finally realized that this person at the wheel holds your life and death in his hands. You didn't choose him. He usurped that power by the nature of his inherited gifts and his education: he can betray you to the enemy, steal your job or wipe out the necessity for the job, change your society with his inventions, destroy the Earth itself."

"Nobody asked for it," Wilson muttered. "Nobody wanted it."

"It was the inevitable result of man's search for truth. Truth is power, and truth is a weapon against society. Society is built on conventions, not truth, and it must protect its vital falsehoods or die. Society is a stable thing. It isn't going anywhere; it is where it's going.

"A society is exactly what it is; it's the only thing it could be under the external and internal forces that acted on it. And whatever it is is good, whatever it does is right and proper, whether it's building pyramids, crucifying an agitator, tearing the breasts off a mother of heretics, or burning witches. Society's function is to protect what it has, to preserve stability above all things."

"But that's static stability," Wilson argued, "and if there's any basic law of the Universe that law is 'Change'!"

"And the creative thinker is the biggest changer of all. He doesn't maintain values; he destroys them as Henry Ford's flivver obsoleted the horse, impoverished the railroads, and developed an entirely new concept of city. The airplane, the atomic powerplant, solar power, something new every day to wipe out the capital investment of another industry, another trade.

"Western culture endured this turmoil for more than two hundred years because of the frontier; change was inevitable, and the creative thinker was useful in making change orderly. But the frontier is gone, and society can no longer afford the creative thinker. He threatens what is, and society cannot tolerate a threat. And so the passenger tries to stop the driver and slow down the car to a speed at which he can jump off."

"And he'll only succeed in wrecking the car and killing them both," Wilson said.

"It's too bad," Pat mused, "that the driver of that car doesn't have a hypodermic under the passenger seat of his car. Then he could anesthetize the passenger and pull over to the side of the road until he could figure out the psychology of this passenger of his, how to control him, and where the devil the car was going. Maybe he could develop a dynamic society that could tolerate creative thinkers because it had dynamic stability, and dynamic security that would keep it from flying all to pieces when change applied speed."

The speaker squealed in Wilson's ear as the girl's thumb touched the car horn. Wilson's body jumped. For a moment he stared at her with startled eyes.

"You—!" he began accusingly, and leaned toward her, his hands lifting toward her throat. Then they would go no higher. His eyelids dropped; he toppled toward her.

She fended him off with one hand and pushed him over against the right hand door. "There now, Dr. Wilson," she murmured, "that didn't hurt much, did it."

Not much, he thought behind closed eyelids, *not much at all. Next time don't warn your victim!*

It was almost noon when they reached New Orleans. As the long, shiny Cadillac coasted to a silent stop at a red light on Tulane Avenue, Wilson leaped over the side of the car and stepped quickly to the sidewalk.

He turned, grinning, and waved at the wide-eyed girl in the Cadillac. "Good-by, Miss Helman. Give my regards to the Senator. And thanks for the ride."

He turned and disappeared into the crowd.

V

Wilson paced the narrow room in the *vieux carré*, paused at the window to stare through the intricate, wrought-iron scrollwork at the rolling, yellow smog, and walked back to the desk. He picked up the paper and read the want-ad once more:

> MEN—between the ages of 25 and 50 for con-
> genial work in South America; excellent sal-
> ary, first-class equipment; knowledge of Span-
> ish or Portuguese helpful but not essential;
> transportation furnished; write to Box 302,
> New Orleans Times-Picayune, listing qualifi-
> cations; replies will be kept confidential.

Wilson threw down the paper impatiently and picked
up the letter beside it. It was addressed to George Mc-
Clure, and it said:

Dear Mr. McClure:

   Your qualifications are impressive, and we would
be most interested in exploring further the possibilities of employing you. There is a small place near
the river known as *Shrimp Heaven.* If you will appear
near this place at 7 P.M. on the 23rd, you will be
given a final interview.

   You need not worry about meeting me. There is
only a handful of men that you could be, and I will
recognize you.

   Come prepared to leave at once if you are accepted.

                                    Until then,
                                    Luis Santoyo

Everything was authentic, from the delicate Latinity of
the phrasing to the characteristic Latin rubrics of the
signature. The want-ad, too, had the ring of truth.

Making contact had been an intellectual puzzle, and
Wilson had worked at it with all his power of concentra-
tion. It was a difficult, dangerous business, this hiring of
scientists and smuggling them out of the country beneath
the noses of the authorities and the Lowbrows. Public
channels were the only method of communication; they
would be minutely watched.

It had been a tense two weeks: finding a place whose
owners needed his rent money too badly to report him,
watching television and the papers, studying the ads.
Some of them were obvious death-traps; others were obviously what they pretended to be. He had discarded them

all but one. That one had differences that were vital to a mind trained to the nuances of meaning.

The age bracket: 25 to 50. Fifty is old for a workman but still young for a creative thinker. "First-class equipment . . . transportation furnished . . . replies confidential." They added up meaningfully.

He shrugged: *all right, it was authentic.* The question was—and now he must face it squarely: *Did he want to leave the United States and go to Brazil or Venezuela or Peru . . . ?*

No, he didn't. Who would want to leave home? And then he thought: *so Einstein hated to leave Germany, so Gamow did not want to leave Russia, so Fermi was reluctant to leave Italy. . . .* Like him they had fled from tyranny, placing the environment of the mind above the environment of the body.

But unlike him they had a country to flee to which did not so much welcome them as admit them and forget them. And inside that country there had been freedom to think and freedom to work, and they had created freely.

What would they have thought of their adopted homeland if they had lived to see it change?

There was no use kidding himself: Brazil was not free nor were any of the other countries that still wanted scientists and technicians. They had frontiers to conquer and new industries to build, but they were going at the job the other way, the planned, heavy-handed way.

But there would be scientists there. They would be working, occasionally, on what they wished. Somehow he would be able to work on the Dictionary and develop the Tool. . . .

And there was no choice when death was on one side.

He turned the paper back to the front page where a long list of names was enclosed in a black-bordered box. Among them were Sylvia Robbins, Aaron Friedman, Samuel Black, and John Wilson. But not William Nugent.

Wilson wondered: had Dr. Nugent been working in Wilson's apartment? Had he been trapped there by the flames?

It might have been a graduate student, but Wilson did not allow himself to hope. Bill Nugent was dead with the others.

It had been a tense two weeks; it had also been a strange two weeks with what another age would have called signs and portents in the heavens. Great showers of meteors had started the night sky with green and yellow and red fireballs and lingering trains, with the rumble of thunder and great explosions heard distantly.

Even this age had reacted to it: a wave of speculation had been followed by a larger wave of superstitious fear. Men did not go out at night if they could help it. Wilson wondered where the meteors had come from: it was too early for the Perseids, and no new comets had been reported.

Wilson slipped into a raincoat and pulled a hat down over his forehead. With his new mustache he was hopeful that a stranger could not identify him from a photograph.

Half an hour later he was watching the decaying, old place on the river called *Shrimp Heaven* on a faded sign above a discolored plate-glass window. The smog was thicker here, rolling in from the river, but when it thinned he could see peeling, gilt letters across the window that spelled: BAR AND GRILL. The back of the building stood on pilings above the roiled, yellow Mississippi.

In the next fifteen minutes nobody entered the place and two persons left: no wonder it was decaying. He was the only one who loitered in the neighborhood.

Wilson crossed the swirling street, smelling the damp rot of the river. As he reached the cracked glass of the revolving door, a man loomed out of the fog toward him.

Light streamed yellowly through the window upon his lined face and iron-gray hair. Wilson started. The speaker buzzed excitedly in his ear. He stepped forward, pushing his hat back to expose his face. "Bill—" he began softly. But the other man's eyes swept over Wilson's face without recognition, and he walked past.

Wilson took a step after him and felt a gentle hand on his arm. In Portuguese a liquid voice said softly, "Professor Nugent is being followed. If you think as much of your own preservation, Professor Wilson, as he does, you will pretend to have dropped something."

Wilson took another step forward; the hand fell away from his arm. Wilson looked down at the sidewalk and bent as if to pick something up. As he stooped, a dark car passed, its headlights cutting yellow cones out of the smog. It stopped just ahead of the tall, lean, iron-gray man.

The back door of the car slid open. A man got out and stood on the sidewalk. He was broad-shouldered and thick-necked. Dr. Nugent tried to go around him, but the man moved again to block his way. He looked down at an object in his hand and back at Dr. Nugent.

Without warning he whipped a big fist into Dr. Nugent's abdomen. Wilson winced, and his fists doubled futilely at his sides. Dr. Nugent doubled up in agony. In swift succession, the man hit him on the back of the neck, raised his knee into Dr. Nugent's face, and hit him in the face as Dr. Nugent reeled back, his face dazed and bloody. He fell against the car and slowly sagged through the door.

The big man on the sidewalk calmly stuffed the legs into the back seat and got in with them. As the door slid shut, the car pulled swiftly away.

The street was silent and empty.

It had happened so quickly that Wilson was still motionless. Now he started forward, but again the hand was a restraint on his arm.

"It is folly to lose two in a futile attempt to save one," said the voice in Portuguese.

Wilson turned. Beside him was a small, dark man of indeterminate age, past his youth certainly and not yet into old age. He was obviously Latin with a dark, little mustache that curled apologetically now. "I am Luis Santoyo," he said. "I regret that I could do nothing for Dr. Nugent."

"Your name isn't Santoyo," Wilson said in fluent Portuguese. "It's Fuentes. I met you in Bogota."

"You have a good memory, Dr. Wilson," the Brazilian said softly. "It would be wise to seek a more secluded spot. I have a room inside."

Wilson nodded briefly and followed the lithe little man through a narrow dining room scattered with a few poorly dressed diners who studiously ignored them. Fuentes skirted a long bar stretched across the back of the room and went through a small door. The room beyond was about eight feet square. Wide floorboards were splintered and bare underfoot. An old fluorescent light flickered and crackled on the ceiling. In the center of the room was a chipped, plastic table and two wrought-iron chairs.

Fuentes shrugged apologetically. "It is ugly but safe.

Sit down, Dr. Wilson, and let us talk of witches and ways to escape the flames."

Wilson looked at him sharply. "Witches?"

"You are a witch, my friend, and that is why the outraged people burned your beautiful university. A few escaped, like you and Dr. Nugent, but you cannot run much farther; you cannot escape without help."

Wilson sank down in one of the chairs and shook his head. "Not witches."

"Why not? Witch is only a variant of the word 'wit'—'to know'—and you are man as knower. Witchcraft is the craft of the wise. The medieval witches and magicians considered themselves scientists, too, you know, and performed their experiments in an attempt to subjugate nature. A witch, my friend, is anyone who has a mysterious power over nature which ordinary mortals cannot attain and who worships gods the people have deserted."

"We worshipped no gods."

"You worshipped the gods of knowledge and truth. They were good for their own sake, you said, regardless of their fruits. But the people deserted those gods a generation ago. They wanted security, not progress; peace of mind, not truth. When a new religion is established in a country, the gods of the old religion become the devils of the new. The devil worshippers, the men of strange powers, become witches, and witches must burn.

"'*Maleficos non patieris vivere*,' says the Bible. 'Thou shalt not suffer a witch to live.'"

Wilson brushed the back of one hand wearily across his forehead. "Perhaps. It is an easy thing to draw parallels, but it is more difficult to find the truth and to recognize it when you have found it. What does Brazil offer a witch?"

"The honor a witch is due," Fuentes said softly, "when his witchcraft is needed. The fear and respect which are the coins of his payment. And the opportunity to continue his subjugation of the universe."

"Freely?" Wilson asked sharply.

Fuentes shrugged. "What is freedom? A relative thing. In Brazil there is freedom to work as one pleases at one's specialty. On the other hand, there are restrictions on what one may publish or say in public which might disturb the people or the orderly processes of government.

But then, as a scientist, you should not be interested in the people or in politics."

"That is what many of us thought," Wilson said quietly, "for too long. In our eagerness to conquer our environment, the universe, we failed to realize until too late that society is part of our environment. As the natural environment lost its power to threaten our existence, society became the most important part. We restricted the ability of fire and flood, of famine, disease, and fanged violence, to kill us—and we transferred their powers to our fellow men. And then society's threat became personal; it was pointed at us. We were not wise; we should have turned our thoughts and investigations toward society; we should have learned how it functions and why."

"These are not proper subjects for investigation," Fuentes said. "If you come to Brazil you will have to forget them."

"We let ourselves be the victims of blind political forces and of demagogues," Wilson went on unchecked. "We should have turned onto sociology and psychology the intense, concentrative techniques of the physical sciences. We might have been able to do what the intuitive psychologists and social scientists failed to do."

"The time for that is long past," Fuentes said. "Nowhere in the world is there a place where you can work at that—not in the African republics or the Chinese empire or the Indian states or Australia. And the witch fever runs stronger in Europe and the U.S.S.R. than here. Once, in the political ignorance of half a century ago, it might have been possible. Not only would it mean that present rulers would lose their power, but a true social science would force changes in human values. And *that* humanity cannot tolerate."

So that hope was gone, too. He had been fleeing, after all, only to save his own life. "Yes," Wilson said, his shoulders drooping wearily, "yes. Too late."

"It is possible," Fuentes said gently, "that this reaction against science is partially due to the increased efforts of science in the social and psychological fields. Intuitive politicians warned you away from politics twice: in the Thirties and in the Fifties. Some of you ignored the warning."

Fuentes looked at Wilson's bent head. "Because you are a great scientist, Dr. Wilson," he said in a brisk, businesslike voice, "Brazil will accept you. But the decision is yours. Will you come?"

Wilson struggled irresolutely. "How do I get there?"

Fuentes pointed beneath the table. "There is a door. Long ago, I understand, it was used during a madness here known as Prohibition. A fast turbine boat waits below. It will speed you to the Gulf, where an atomic submarine waits."

Wilson sighed helplessly. "Let's go."

Together they lifted the plastic table aside. Fuentes knelt on the floor and felt for a handle.

In his ear, the speaker began to scream. Wilson said: "Hurry up! There is danger close."

Fuentes looked up, puzzled, shook his head, and lifted a square door. Beneath it was blackness. Smog drifted dankly up into the room. "Go down, my friend. There is a ladder on this side."

The speaker intensified its shrill warnings of violent theta waves not far away. Wilson lowered himself hesitantly into the hole, his feet groping. He found the rung and went down swiftly until his feet hit a swaying platform.

Strong hands grabbed his arms and held them tightly. A flashlight blazed up into Fuentes' suddenly pale face.

"Thanks, spick," said a harsh voice beside Wilson's ear. "We wanted this one. The Senator will be very happy."

Wilson struggled, but the hands holding him were strong. The boat swayed under his feet.

"Quiet, Wilson," the voice grated at him, "or we'll have to quiet you."

Wilson stopped fighting and looked up at Fuentes. The Brazilian's face was twisted and angry. "You must release this man," Fuentes said in shrill English. "The Brazilian government has extended to him its protection."

"To a criminal?" the man in the boat mocked. "To a convicted arsonist? No, Fuentes, that won't do."

Fuentes shook with passion, staring down into the light. "This is an insult to the Brazilian government. We will not let it go unpunished."

"Any time," the voice said dryly. "Be glad we don't take you along, little man, and drop you into the river with an anchor tied to your feet."

Slowly the passion left Fuentes' face. He looked down wistfully toward Wilson. "You knew that there was danger close," he said quietly. "Almost I think you are a witch, after all. I hope you are. You will need all your craft."

"So long, Fuentes," the voice said. "Send us some more."

The light flicked off. In the darkness, the boat began to move silently away. As it shoved into the grayness above the river, Wilson was pulled down hard onto a seat thinly padded with foam rubber. Rope was twisted tightly around his wrists; they were tied to something behind him.

Before his fingers became too numb, he felt it; it was a cleat fastened to the side of the boat. He tugged at it, but it was solid. The possibility of jumping overboard was gone.

The boat picked up speed in the river, the only sound the bubbling of the water jet behind; it glided through the fog without running lights. "Well, Wilson," the harsh voice said, "you ran a long way to fall right into our arms."

"I gave you a chase, anyway," Wilson said wearily.

"What chase? Who followed you? We knew you'd head for a port; so we waited for you. We know all the recruiters; we read their mail and bug their offices and favorite meeting spots. Once in a while we let them smuggle out a small-timer just so they don't get discouraged. But we wanted you and Nugent here. You're the fall guys for the great Egghead Plot."

"Nugent? Here?"

"Yeah. But he ain't in any condition to talk."

There was suddenly a slight wave of heat. It played over Wilson for a moment, and he heard a sound in the air like the flutter of leathery wings. Out of the smog drifted a red ball of fire and then a second one. They touched the radar antenna and clung there, one above the other, lighting up the boat with a dim, reddish radiance.

Wilson had seen it before: *witch fire.*

Wilson was vaguely surprised to notice that the man opposite him was not thin and dark-haired. He was the broad-shouldered hoodlum who had beaten Dr. Nugent.

He had a machine pistol in his hands, but it was forgotten. He was staring over his shoulder at the brush discharge of electricity. "What did Fuentes mean—'witch'?" he asked harshly, swinging around.

"Don't you know?" Wilson's voice was deep. "I can call down the lightning bolt from heaven; I can call forth the fire from the earth. I can bring life to the dying and death to the living. I can take your warped mind and make it sound again."

"Don't make jokes!" The voice was uneasy.

The phone, which had quieted, began to buzz louder in Wilson's ear. That was fear. By bringing fire and violence against scientists, the Lowbrow had endowed them in the secret recesses of his mind with a power to match his measures.

"No joke," Wilson said. The ball lightning began to fade as its charge leaked away. "In my mind is the power to build a city or to smash one flat, to send a spear crashing through the sky or to bring a star so close you can almost reach out and touch it, to make man as wealthy and as powerful as the ancient gods or to make him a beggar among untouchable wealth. I am all-powerful; I am Man the Witch, the seeker after mysteries, the knower of all things, the doer to whom nothing is sacred, nothing too difficult—"

"Shut up!" said the hoodlum. The witch fire had disappeared; in the darkness Wilson listened to the Lowbrow's theta rhythms, violent and swift, and waited. "No wonder the Senator says you're all traitors," the Lowbrow said, swearing crudely. "No wonder he says you got to die. You don't care about people or the U.S. or anything. All you care about is your laboratories and your experiments, and let the devil take the hindmost."

"As he will take you, my friend," Wilson said quietly.

The man cursed savagely. There was a whisper of movement in the darkness. The earphone squealed in an ascending scale. Wilson was waiting. As the Lowbrow lunged, Wilson's foot caught him in the face. Cartilage yielded as he shoved. As the man hurtled backward, Wilson felt a deep, atavistic surge of savage satisfaction.

Somewhere forward, metal tore tinnily. Feet moved in the darkness.

Wilson was yanking at the cord, but he succeeded only in cutting it into the flesh of his wrists. His hands got wet and slippery, but the rope held them tight.

Something was hovering in the darkness above. Wilson had a vague sensation of heat, and then he heard a thin tinkling of broken glass. Wilson caught a whiff of something acrid and sulphurous before he stopped breathing.

He held his breath as long as he could. When he had to release it, the odor was gone. Something thumped lightly to the deck near him.

In a moment he felt fingers plucking at the rope that held his wrists. They stopped briefly.

"Ugh!" said a feminine voice. "Blood!"

"What did you expect," Wilson asked impatiently, "ice water?"

"Your old self, eh, Dr. Wilson?"

Something sawed at the ropes. "What was that sulphurous stink?" he growled.

"A fast-acting anesthetic. Quick thinking to hold your breath. Actually the fire-and-brimstone was gratuitous. Just for effect."

"Like the St. Elmo's fire?"

"Yes. We have a generator."

The ropes fell away from his wrists. Wilson flexed them experimentally and decided they would still work. "Dr. Nugent is aboard somewhere."

"Let's find him."

A hand found his and led him forward in the darkness. "How are you getting around?" he asked. "Infrared?"

"Exactly. Some more of the mumbo-jumbo. Just a minute. Here's the man you kicked. He isn't very pretty. But then he wasn't very pretty to start with."

The girl had stopped. She released his hand. There was a sharp, little hiss in the darkness.

"What was that?" Wilson asked.

"Hypodermic," she said briefly. "Make certain he stays asleep until we get away. Also induces an innocuous but uncomfortable and long-lasting disease resembling shingles. And, incidentally, tattooes him with a witch's mark—to his grave. He will swear that you and Dr. Nugent are dead. In his world that's the only way he and the others can survive."

"Who are you anyway?" Wilson asked as she took his hand again and led him forward, twisting through a narrow doorway and into a cabin. Twice more he heard the brief hiss of the hypodermic.

"We're witches," she said lightly. "Like you."

"Seriously," Wilson insisted.

"Very seriously," she replied. "The day of the scientist in the free society is gone; we must be witches in another kind of society. Here's Dr. Nugent. Can you carry him?"

Wilson slipped his hands under the man lying unconscious in what felt like a bunk. He lifted him and held him against his chest. Nugent's body was heavy but not as heavy as Wilson had expected. The long chase had gaunted him.

"Your voice is familiar," Wilson said, frowning. "I should know you."

"You should," she agreed and guided him by an elbow.

"Why should I trust you?"

"Are we back to that again? she asked impatiently. "What else can you do?"

"The girl in the Cadillac," Wilson said suddenly. "Pat Helman."

"The same."

"You aren't alone."

"No. There are a few others, some scientists, some laymen, but eggheads all. A decade ago some of them decided that the pressing need for research was in society itself. They didn't learn much, but they learned enough to know that it was time to hide: The Lowbrow movement—whatever its name—was inevitable."

"Did they do anything except hide?"

"You've just seen what they have done. They have begun the creation of a myth. The Lowbrow movement can't be stopped, but it can be guided—with skill and luck. Instead of the disintegration of civilization, there will be a slowing down. Instead of smashing up the car, Dr. Wilson, we're going to brake it. We're going to pull it over to the side of the road and figure out how to control the passenger and how to make the steering mechanism work.

"Here's a stretcher," she said briskly. "Put Dr. Nugent in it."

There were ropes at the four ends of the stretcher. As soon as Wilson lowered Nugent's body onto the canvas, it was whispered away.

"In a generation," the girl said, "cities will cease to exist as social and economic entities. Men will stop using industrial machinery; no one will be able to make it or to keep it in repair. The population will plummet during an interregnum of starvation and violence. If we are successful, the people who are left will live in small, self-supporting communities. Witches will live among them, part of them, helping and learning."

"You talk very glibly for an errand girl," Wilson said dryly.

"Hanging around eggheads, you pick it up. Besides, where can you go? You can stay here with Sleeping Ugly or you can climb this ladder with me."

She put a snaky, metal rung in his hand. He took a deep breath. "What can I lose?" he said. He started up the ladder. It swayed under him.

The leathery swish was loud as he came through an open hatch into the body of the helicopter. By the dim radiance from a strip of fluorescent paint circling the narrow cabin, he saw a hand extended to help him up.

It pulled him close to a face he had been expecting: the face of a thin, dark-haired man he had seen three times before—once in a hotel lobby, once outside an electronic parts store, and once in the doorway of a railway bedroom.

Irony: the man he had been evading was help, and he had run away from him and run straight into the hands of the Lowbrows.

Wilson dropped the hand and pulled back toward the side of the ship, feeling a vague distaste for all this mummery; mixed up in it was a feeling of disillusion about his own judgment. The ship was rising, which meant there was a third person, a pilot, forward.

Beside the open hatch in the helicopter's belly was the stretcher. On it was Dr. Nugent, breathing stertorously, his face bruised and stained with blood.

Through the hatch came Pat. She was wearing a conical hat and a black robe. Heavy goggles masked her eyes, and a hooked nose drooped toward a fanged mouth.

"Laugh, damn it!" she said. "This isn't my idea." She stripped off the goggles and the nose and removed the fangs; once more she was merely a very pretty girl.

Not *"merely,"* Wilson thought. Certainly not *merely.*

"I think it's going too far," Pat said.

Wilson didn't feel like laughing. "All right. The masquerade is over; it's time to unmask. Who are you?"

"Witches," said the dark-haired man. "If you want a personal handle, it's Pike. But that isn't important now. The question is: who are you?"

VI

An angry pulse began to beat in Wilson's temple. He had run too far and too fast and too long. "You know who I am!"

"Dr. John Wilson, associate professor of psychology, who knows everything and has learned nothing?"

Wilson stared at Pike blankly. The man was serious. "What are you talking about?"

"You," Pike said calmly. "You just can't admit that you were wrong, can you? That you were a fool, that you were mistaken?"

"Wrong?" Wilson repeated. "I thought your purpose was to rescue me from the Lowbrows. Was I wrong about that?"

"Yes. Our purpose was to rescue you from yourself. But we make mistakes, too. We can deliver you to Fuentes' sub. Is that what you want—to run to Brazil?"

Wilson ran his tongue over dry lips. "There's no alternative, is there?"

"Consistently Aristotelian, aren't you, Dr. Wilson? With you it must always be alternatives: black or white; good or bad; run and live or stay and die. . . ."

"It boils down to that," Wilson said coldly. His temper was back under control. The long flight and the long peril had worn his nerves thin; he thought he had found friends, that he could relax. That was his mistake. These people were scheming maniacs playing on the superstitions of morons. "A man who refuses to choose a side is a coward."

"And a man who chooses a side without recognizing that he is probably wrong is a fool. You can't choose sides against humanity. The human problems must be lived with. You're a fool, John Wilson, and worse—you're a fool who knows he is right, who is sure that he has the Answers if They will only listen. You're no different from the Lowbrows. You haven't learned anything, and you don't want to learn."

Wilson's hand touched the cabin wall behind him. It was real and solid, not dream stuff. "If that's what you think of me, you went to a lot of trouble to get me away from the Lowbrows." Even to himself, his voice sounded plaintive and rejected.

Pike shrugged. "Life isn't mathematics, and the rules aren't interchangeable. You can't add two and two and get four in human values. To make a worthwhile member of the human race is equal to whatever effort is necessary."

"Go to hell!" Wilson growled. "Nobody asked to be saved."

"Still sure you're right, aren't you? Still sure the mob that burned the university was wrong. After everything that has happened to you, you haven't rearranged a hair of one of your beliefs."

"Why should I?"

Pike studied him as if Wilson were a specimen under his microscope. "Because you're wrong, John Wilson. You're as wrong as Senator Bartlett, who acted out of his convictions, too. You think that because you're a little brainier than the Lowbrows your convictions are superior; it isn't true. Because you can manipulate a few people, because you taunted that poor Lowbrow in the boat into jumping you, you think that you know people. Nuts, Dr. Wilson! Senator Bartlett knows more about people than you will ever know. He accepts them for what they are, and he manipulates them by the millions. By any standard, you are a failure."

Wilson glanced helplessly at Pat. In her eyes he read something he did not want: a deep, impotent pity. Quickly he looked back at Pike and something he could face.

"You blame the Lowbrow because he wants security more than truth," Pike said evenly. "But nobody wants security more than you do. You want the world to admit how right you are, no matter what the truth is—because then you won't have to change your beliefs. The Lowbrow seeks his security in human convictions and faiths and strong attachments; you seek your security in the assurance of Absolute Law. Both are static; both are equally deadly.

"There are no Absolute Laws in human affairs, Dr. Wilson. There are only eternal variables. A static philosophy and a static society cannot contain them. For a little while they will compress humanity until, warped and twisted, humanity bursts the molds."

"You have all the answers, don't you?" Wilson snapped angrily.

"We don't have any of them. We have only the answers that failed. The Universities were one of them. They had to burn; they earned it."

"You're mad; utterly mad!"

"Too long they served as fortresses of isolation, walling in the learned man, the eggheads of yesterday and today, insulating them from humanity and its problems. What you were doing was so much more important than the problems of the little man who kept tugging at your sleeve, trying to get your attention. Finally he had to try something else. He gave you exactly the kind of trouble he had: insecurity and the fear of sudden death. Maybe, his instincts said, he could learn something from your efforts to solve the problem.

"He was wrong. Your only solution was to run, seeking a place where the lightning had not struck, where the fortresses were still unbroken. You couldn't learn to live with this new situation and adjust your convictions to this new reality. And you ran, angry at the impatient child who had a temper tantrum, unable to recognize that it was your fault for provoking a temper tantrum in someone inherently incapable of patience."

"Sylvia Robbins died in that temper tantrum," Wilson said unsteadily, rage shaking his voice.

"Sylvia Robbins had to die. And Aaron Friedman and Sammy Black and a hundred others. You can't make an omelette without breaking a few eggheads. The eggheads sealed themselves into shells, and they had to be broken out. They were kicked out because they didn't have the guts to do it themselves.

"As an evolutionary experiment, the Scientist's isolation was an expensive failure. Nature has a way of scrapping failures. The eggheads are being scrapped now so that the components can be used for more valuable organisms."

Wilson's control snapped. He swung forward, his hands doubled into fists. "You son of a—"

Pike's fist was there first. For Wilson the thin, fluorescent strip jiggled and blurred and went out.

When Wilson opened his eyes, he was on the floor of

the helicopter, his head cradled in something soft and alive. It was Pat Helman's lap.

Pike was standing above him, fingering his jaw reminiscently. "I can be human, too," he said wryly.

Wilson brought his arm up over his eyes and pressed it down hard, fighting to keep himself intact. The most terrible sound in the world is the shattering of a lifelong set of values at the touch of reality.

For the first time Wilson looked at the facts straight-on, not refracted through the imperfect prism of his convictions: his values had not been able to save the university. If Pike was right, they had carried the torch to it themselves. They had led him right into the hands of the Lowbrows, and in the crucial test, they had broken, just as the Lowbrow's control had broken in the boat below.

That he had been knocked out was immaterial. That he had turned to force was an admission that his beliefs were unable to survive the first verbal attack. And his subconscious knew it.

Wilson groaned and pulled his arm away. He looked up at Pike. "If the world we have is no good, if the age of science has failed," he asked, "what have you got to take its place?"

Pike shrugged helplessly. "We don't know enough to tell you. We don't even know what we need in order to know. New facts, perhaps, or a new way of thinking about the facts we have. But I'll tell you what we offer: a chance at a world without security, a world in which insecurity is accepted as the right and proper state of man, a world in which death is certain, in which the only constant is man's determination that death shall not be in vain and that the life before that death shall be a challenge—for challenge is inescapable by the nature of the universe."

Wilson sat up, and his mind shattered into brittle shards of pain. "What crazy kind of a world is that?"

"The world that is coming, inevitably. As witches perhaps we can shorten to a century or so the millennial grinding of the millstones of the universe."

"A world of poverty and superstition?" Wilson sneered. "If that's the world that's coming, I'd rather not live to see it."

"Perhaps so," Pike said soberly. "It takes a great courage to face an uncertain future, even more when the future may bring a complete reversal of all your convictions, must surely bring it, when you will have to change your basic beliefs and work for ways of life you learned to hate with your mother's milk."

"How will you escape the flames?"

"Today scientist-witches are burned because the uncertainty of the age demands scapegoats. Self-doubt breeds self-hate and uncertainty breeds brutality. In the burning of the witch a social poison is excreted; the witch dies for the people.

"In time men will learn to live with uncertainty because they must, and then the witch-scientist will be restored to his ancient position and his ancient authority: the wise man of the village, who wields mysterious control over the forces of nature—for the benefit of the village. Witchcraft will be an integral part of the social inheritance; it will be what it once was—a search for truth in an uncertain world.

"But the scientist-witch must burn. He hasn't learned anything in three hundred years; no, not in three hundred centuries. His reaction to danger is still the reaction of the dawn man: fight or flight."

Wilson frowned, trying to straighten out his thoughts. "What do you want me to do?" he said in a low voice.

Pike looked at Pat for a moment and sighed. "Come down out of your ivory tower, Dr. Wilson. Become plain John Wilson, an ordinary, struggling, suffering citizen. Try living with the great problem of our day, not fighting it or running from it. Find out how the people think, but more important, how they feel and hate and love.

"And when you have learned that much, perhaps you will have learned what you can do to make their lives— and yours—more successful."

"Live with the Lowbrows?" Wilson repeated incredulously.

"More," Pike said. "Be one of them. Force yourself to admit their viewpoint into your understanding. Discover, as a psychologist, what your patient really is and how to cure him, rather than demanding that the patient be some hypothetical patient you can cure. Try to understand why the witch-burner and the witch are children of the same confusion, fathered by the same inner necessity. Learn to sympathize with the emotional need for scapegoats in an era of bewilderment when old ways of life are failing."

"I'll be caught!" Wilson exclaimed.

"Not if you really become a Lowbrow. What about it, John Wilson? Do you have the guts to admit you might be wrong, that you could learn something that would change your view of the universe, perhaps your way of life?"

Wilson hauled himself to his feet. Past the curved, plastic window, trailing fingers of fog thinned and then were gone. The night was clear; the stars were brilliant and hard in the blackness. As Wilson watched, one of the stars fell and streaked across the horizon like a green ball of flame, leaving behind it a fading train.

But it was not that easy for Wilson to climb above the fog and see the stars. *Perhaps he was wrong. If failure is the consequence of wrong ideas and disaster, of incorrect convictions, he was wrong.*

But knowing it intellectually and realizing it emotionally were quite different things.

Could he face the fact that he might be wrong, as wrong as the Lowbrows? Could he take the chance that he might one day admit it—and be forced to change or die?

Did he have the guts to take his convictions in his hand and cast them out and see how they fell?

Blindly Wilson reached out for strength and understanding. He found Pat's hand.

He clung to it desperately, the only solid thing in a Protean world.

VII

Three months and five shattered universities later, a man in work-stained clothing walked along the top of a hill that had once housed knowledge, and the ashes were ugly and black on either side of him. He descended the steep sidewalk, alone, and reached Massachusetts Street and walked north.

He had no illusions about what he was going to do. It was a hard, bitter road he was about to walk, and everyone would line the road to stone him, eggheads and

Lowbrows, scientists and laymen. Death might lie at the end of it, and it would be an ugly, brutal death as such occasions always are.

But he knew, now, why the people needed scapegoats, and only at the end of the road could he find the truth about himself.

He turned east one block. He went through the doorway of the old, brick police building and found a room where a uniformed police officer sat behind a desk.

"My name is John Wilson," he said evenly. "I think you are looking for me."

PART TWO

TRIAL BY FIRE

I

"The people against John Wilson," a man said. It was chanted like an incantation, and it echoed in his head. "The people against John Wilson. The people against John Wilson."

John Wilson. John Wilson. Then he remembered. He was John Wilson. He tried to open his eyes and found they were open. Slowly, as he tried to remember what he had been doing before this moment, where he had been, who he was, his surroundings swam into focus.

He was in a large room with a high ceiling. He was conscious of the size before he saw it. Varnished wood was slick under his hands. He was seated in a wooden arm chair at a long wooden table. The wood was light-colored, oak perhaps. Opposite him was another long table. Two men sat on the other side of it, facing him. One was a big, blocky man with light brown hair and lumpy features. The other was smaller and younger. He had a large nose and dark, curly hair that grew low on his forehead. His lips seemed set in a perpetual sneer, and his close-set, black eyes squinted now at Wilson, looking into Wilson's eyes speculatively, sardonically.

Wilson stared back. He wondered why this young man was so interested in him. Did the young man know him? Did he know the young man?

Another voice was speaking. "John Wilson, please stand," it said. The voice had said the same thing before.

"Can you stand up?" asked a voice beside him. The voice was light and drawling, with an edge of irony.

Wilson put his hands on the arms of the chair and

pushed himself erect. It was no particular effort, but once
he was up the room spun around him in a blur of alter-
nating darkness and light. The illusion reminded him of a
carousel ride when he was young, and he watched it with
interest and nostalgia.

As the room began to slow and settle into place, he
saw a man placed higher than he was some ten paces to
his right. The man was seated behind a tall, broad desk-
like piece of furniture. The front of it was made of oak,
too, and it was carved into patterns of rectangles within
rectangles. The desk had two levels, with lower sections
at each end. Behind the man was a section of carved oak
paneling against a painted wall. The paneling was topped
with fluted molding, four knobs, and a wooden eagle. The
green paint on the wall was peeling.

The man behind the desk leaned forward. He had gray,
wavy hair and a triangular face. "I say again, John Wilson," he said, "you are accused of arson and of murder
in the first degree. How do you plead?"

"Arson?" Wilson thought. "Murder?" Had he burned
something? Killed somebody? He could not remember. He
could remember flames, yes, flames roaring in the night
and forked, black figures running back and forth. And he
could remember a silent crowd that waited for the figures
with clubs and pitchforks and axes, and some of the
black figures chose the flames. But it was more like the
memory of a nightmare than of something real. And it
had for him the spectatorlike quality of a dream. Was it
reality instead, something he had pushed into the subconscious through fear or guilt?

The drawling voice beside him helped. "My client
pleads not guilty," it said.

"Thank you, Mr. Youngman," said the man behind the
desk. Only it was not a desk, of course. It was a bench,
and the man was a judge.

He was being tried for arson and murder, Wilson told
himself, and he couldn't remember what he had done or
what had brought him here or, now that he thought about
it, anything of his past. Was he a victim of amnesia? Of
course not. There was no such thing as amnesia. Of that
he was sure. Only he didn't know why he was sure.

Wilson sank back into his chair, thankful he had been
relieved of the compulsion to speak, thankful, too, that

someone had believed in him enough to speak up for his innocence.

His heart overflowing with warmth, Wilson turned his head to the left. Seated beside him was a tall, thin man with short, sandy hair and a face like a beardless Lincoln. His long legs were curled under his chair, and his body was curled, too, until it rested on its spine. He was cadaverously thin, but his face was tanned and his indolent body seemed coiled with wiry strength. He smiled at Wilson and nodded as if to say, "You don't need to say anything. We're in this together, you and I."

Or so Wilson interpreted it, with relief, partly because he did not know what to say, partly because he was not sure he could muster the will to speak.

Men and women were being questioned, one at a time, as they sat in a chair on a platform raised a foot above the floor on the right of the judge's bench. The women seemed much alike and so did the men. The women were dressed in long dark dresses of gray or black or dark blue cotton, the men in coveralls with blue shirts or occasionally a dark suit with a blue shirt underneath open at the throat. So, too, were dressed the men at the table opposite him. One of them was not at the table now. He was asking questions of the men and women who sat in the chair. The younger one sat at the table. He said nothing. He stared at Wilson or occasionally allowed his gaze to drift around the room.

The questioning had been going on for some time now, Wilson decided. He must have drifted away again because half the chairs facing him in front of the oak partition now were filled with men and women. Like the young man at the table, they spent most of their time looking at him.

"Do you have a financial interest in any scientific laboratory?" the blocky man was asking. "Has any member of your family attended college? Taught in college? Performed research? Has any member of your family benefited from any of the so-called miracle treatments for organic disease? Do any of them have artificial organs?"

"Objection!" Youngman said occasionally.

"Overruled," said the judge.

If the answer to any of his questions was "yes," the blocky man said, "You are dismissed," and if the answer to all of them was "no," he would turn to Youngman with a little bow, and Youngman would uncoil himself and standing negligently beside the table asking idle questions. He was not content to ask the same questions over and over like the blocky man. He asked some of the men and women whether they had made up their minds about the case, some whether they had seen the university burn, some whether they knew the defendant, and one whether he had any prejudices about science or scientists.

"Objection, your honor," said the blocky man.

"Sustained," said the judge, and he turned to Youngman to say, "I must warn you, Counselor, that this line of questioning is not permissible. Science is not on trial here nor are scientists."

"Exception," said Youngman. "The clerk will note the fact as grounds for appeal. Science and scientists are on trial here, as they are throughout this nation and throughout the world. Universities are being burned; scientists are being hunted down and exterminated. . . ."

"I must caution you, Counselor, that you are risking contempt proceedings with this outburst," the judge said.

"I will call attention to the irregularities of this trial," Youngman said, "as the basis for an appeal not only to a higher court but to a higher jury." He waved his hand toward the back of the room. "There is the proof of the nature of this trial. . . ."

"If you do not control yourself I will also dismiss you from this case," the judge said.

Wilson let his attention wander. To his left was a wooden railing. In the railing were three wooden gates on hinges, one at either side of him and one behind him where the railing jogged to allow room for a doorway with double doors into the courtroom.

Beyond the railing was the audience. They sat in pew-like benches. They sat silently in their dark dresses and their blue shirts, their hands folded in their laps or their arms folded across their chests. They stared at him. Wilson could not read their expressions, whether it was judgment suspended or judgment passed. If he was an arsonist and a murderer they would hate him, of course. Good men and women hate evil.

Here and there in the audience were a few persons who did not seem to fit with the rest—a beautiful blond girl with short hair, young men with hard faces and watchful eyes, a few men in uniform on the front row and at the door.

Behind the audience, at the back of the two aisles, were the television cameras pointed at the front of the room, at the men and women in the witness chair or at the lawyers or at the judge or at someone behind Wilson, but mostly at Wilson himself. He amused himself with watching the little red eye beneath the long lenses, particularly when he could tell that the lens was pointing toward him.

The blocky man—what had the judge called him? Oh, yes, the district attorney—was talking to the jury, but he kept turning toward the television cameras. The twelve chairs for the jury were placed in two rows of six; they all were filled. Above them was a crowded balcony. The balcony was reached by a narrow corridor behind the paneled partition that formed the back of the jury box and by a circular staircase at the end of the corridor. In the balcony were people who kept pointing things at him.

The district attorney was saying, "I shall prove that this man, in league with others like him, planned the burning of the University to discredit the Lowbrow Party and the Senate Subcommittee on Academic Practices and in an attempt to gain sympathy for the egghead cause . . . that the fire got out of hand and killed many of the arsonists themselves, but that this man, John Wilson, escaped and made his way to the Gulf Coast, where he attempted to sell his services and his nation's secrets to a foreign power and where he was captured by courageous members of this nation's national police force and returned to the Federal Penitentiary to stand trial. . . ."

There was no doubt, Wilson thought. The expression of the audience was hate. Before the scene faded out he decided that he liked the other dream better. As this one ended he felt Youngman take him by the hand in farewell. Then he was in some kind of wheeled vehicle. From the vibration he thought it was moving fast. He was lying flat on a kind of cot. On the other side was another cot. Someone was sitting on it. In a moment he recognized the dark-haired young man from the courtroom.

"He keeps coming out of it," the young man said with an eastern accent. His voice had a sneer to it, too. "Give him a bigger dose."

Someone leaned over him, shutting off his view of the young man, and he felt something cold and metallic placed against his bare arm. He heard a hissing noise, and the cold object went away. He turned on his left side and let his eyelids descend. After a suitable period he tried to read the note Youngman had pressed into his hand. The light through the barred window beside him flickered, but he finally made out the words.

"You're under some kind of sedation. Next time try to cut yourself. We'll analyze the blood. Destroy the note. It's soluble in water."

How interesting, Wilson thought. He worked his hand up to his mouth and slipped the paper between his lips. It dissolved all right. It tasted like peppermint.

II

He woke in the transparent darkness just before dawn. Someone was hammering at the door. "Doctor," the door murmured through the house. "Doctor." He got up quickly and slipped into his white coat. He never appeared to the villagers like an ordinary man; that would corrode their confidence.

When he reached the door, it transmitted to him the voice of an excited woman. "Doctor, my little girl!" And more knocking.

He pressed a button beside the door, as he ran his fingers through his hair. It was the blond Pat Helman, as he had thought. He could see her plainly in the mirror beside the door. She had her daughter in her arms. They were alone.

Wilson took a stimulant pill from the dispenser beside the door, shook off the last remnants of his disturbed slumber, and told the door to open. "Come in," he said to the woman.

He took the little girl from her mother and carried her into the laboratory, shutting the door of the white-tiled room carefully in the mother's face. The girl was hot and breathing rapidly but still conscious. He placed the girl on the diagnostic table and set the dials for her identification.

The computer clicked as it searched its memory bank for the girl's medical history. The sensors applied themselves to the girl's body while Wilson soothed her fears with a calm hand and a calmer voice. In a moment the diagnosis appeared in the frosted glass above the little girl's head. Encephalitis. The injection came immediately afterward, painlessly, virtually unfelt.

Wilson returned the girl to her mother. "She'll be all right now," he said confidently. "But hang this around her neck to ward off evil." It was a simple puzzle, and perhaps the girl would improve her mind.

"Thank you, doctor, thank you, thank you," the young woman said, unable to stop. "She would have died."

"Yes," Wilson said. She would have, too, he thought. "How is your husband's leg?"

"All healed. He was walking on it the next day, just as if it had never been broken."

"And does he remember to say the charm?"

"The two-times-two? Yes, Doctor. I'm even beginning to say it, as well, just from hearing it so often."

"It won't hurt you," Wilson said. "You missed much instruction, coming from the city."

"We'll bring you a pig, Doctor!"

"I am here to help. Is everything all right in the village?"

"The stranger is still at the motel. The one we suspect is a tax collector. He has been asking questions about you."

"By name?"

"No. He asks only about our witch-doctor. Are you good? Do you charge too much? Where do you live? Do you have visitors? We do not tell him anything."

"Thank you, my dear."

He did not have time to think about the stranger in the village. Scarcely had the door closed behind Pat Helman and her daughter than the knocking began again and the door announced other callers.

First it was a farmer whose corn was not growing as it should in spite of fertilizer and water. He brought a sample of soil. The analyzer said it was too acid, and Wilson gave him a wagonload of holy powder to work into the land. A delivery truck limped in for service. The analyzer revealed that the reactor element was worn out and would have to be replaced and sent in for renewal. Even with the automatic equipment in the sealed garage, the job took half an hour.

Then came the most difficult part of Wilson's job, the birth of a child with a brain injury. The diagnosis was quick and the reaction immediate. The child was dead as soon as the computer clicked out the judgment that it would never lead more than a vegetable existence. Wilson found the mother's gratitude most difficult to endure, but he knew it was deserved.

By this time the sun was well up, and the time for religious instruction was at hand. In the classroom was a sprinkling of children from four to sixteen, and even a few married women who could not go on the pilgrimage and were not yet tied down by children. He welcomed them all.

After an invocation and a brief sermon, Wilson settled them to their individual programs at their individual learning stations, and soon they were listening to the individual instruction that seemed to come to them out of the air. They listened for a few minutes, wrote on the magic tablets in front of them, and then compared their answers with the one in the soothsayer window beside the tablet.

Wilson left them and returned to his living quarters in the self-contained cottage. Now he would have a few moments of rest with everyone at work in their homes or in the fields or in the classroom. Perhaps he would even have time for a little research of his own.

But he did not have the time after all. He had no more settled himself into his favorite chair in the study than the computer told him that someone had followed him from the classroom and was trying to unscrew the inspection post on the computer. He opened the door.

"Hello, Christopher," he said.

It was the James boy—17 years old and a good student, a handsome, quick, inquisitive lad with an annoying habit of arguing with his elders that caused dissension in the village. His parents despaired of making him a cooperating part of the family group.

But he was sullen now.

"Well," Wilson said.

"I wish to be a wise man like you," the boy said.

"How like me?" Wilson asked.

"Wise like you. I wish to know all things."

"I do not know all things. The universe is infinite and eternal, and even if a man searched through infinity for an eternity still he would not know all things."

"I wish then to know as much as a man can know."

"Knowledge alone is neither a blessing or a virtue."

"It is all I want."

"The passion for knowledge is a fever that can consume a man."

"I am consumed. How can I learn more?"

"There is the classroom."

"The voice of God tells me only what I know already. It is drill only, and I do it perfectly."

That was true, Wilson knew. The boy had made no mistakes for weeks. The computer had warned him that it was time for the boy to begin his pilgrimage. "Knowledge is worthless without an end. The idle learner is a danger not only to himself but to others. He will put his knowledge to work only to satisfy his idle curiosity, heedless of the consequences, as you have done here."

The boy argued. "This surely is man's destiny—to seek truth and to follow wherever it leads. Truth is the greatest good. If some are hurt in the discovery, some always will be hurt—in its absence even more than in its presence—and it is better that they be hurt in the search for truth than in the protection of their ignorance."

"The man who has found true wisdom does not deal in right and wrong; he does not judge ends. For some, truth is a good, for others, a god. It must be good for all or it is good for none. God must serve man, not man God. The latter way leads to cruelty and amorality justified by self-righteousness."

"How can truth be good for all?" Christopher asked sullenly.

"I have sought truth all my life," said Wilson. "How do I use the little I have found?"

"You serve the village, but—"

"Yes?"

The boy burst out, "What good is knowledge if one cannot seek more, if with every step one cannot see the universe opening up?"

Wilson was silent. He let the boy think about it.

"I suppose," Christopher said reluctantly, "you do not

stop seeking. But you spend time in service when you might be learning." He was silent again. "I suppose I could learn to serve."

"That is part of what you must learn," Wilson said.

"How do I start?"

"The way of the seeker after truth is long and difficult," Wilson warned him.

The boy nodded. He did not know, Wilson thought, he could not know how hard and how difficult it was, but perhaps, perhaps, he would follow the path to its end.

"You have lived in this village long enough," Wilson said. "Now you must go out and learn something about the world. You will wander from place to place learning about people and serving them, doing for them what they cannot do for themselves, and learning to do it with a glad heart. Perhaps you may spend some time at the Emperor's Court. Perhaps you may visit another kingdom. But if you learn well and seek long, you may find the way to greater knowledge than you now dream of, knowledge you do not need to steal."

"When can I begin?" the boy asked.

"Ask your parents," Wilson said gently. "Tell them I said you are ready for the pilgrimage." They would be sorry to see the boy go, he thought, and yet relieved.

The boy turned eagerly toward the door and then swung back. "Will I ever be like you, Doctor?"

"If you seek long and are found worthy, you will learn much. One day, if you are successful in all things, you will be expected to serve as I do."

"May I be worthy," the boy said.

As he left, the door admitted George Johnson, the village elder. He was breathless with excitement. "Doctor," he said, panting. "There are soldiers in the village."

"How many?"

"Eight and a sergeant. They are demanding taxes."

"They or the stranger?"

"The stranger. He commands them."

"Where are they?"

"At the motel. Shall we refuse to pay? Shall we resist?"

" 'Render unto Caesar what is Caesar's.' But I will go to speak with them."

When he reached the motel, he found two soldiers in imperial purple guarding the door with their pellet guns.

They stirred uneasily at the sight of his white jacket and then stood aside to admit him.

At a table in the dining room, a man in a wrinkled suit and an open-collared blue shirt was accepting a few pieces of gold jewelry from one of the villagers and checking off a name on a list. The man looked up and an expression of sardonic delight crossed his face as he waved the villager away.

The man was out of Wilson's persistent nightmare. He had dark, curly hair that grew low on his forehead, a large nose, and close-set black eyes that looked speculatively into Wilson's.

"You have come."

"You state the obvious."

"The rest is incidental," the young man said. "Worthwhile but incidental. We wished only to get you away from your fortress. We have had quite enough of their defenses."

"Here I am," Wilson said. "If you are on a witch-hunt, you have found someone who will serve your purpose."

"You will be taken to district court for trial."

Wilson nodded.

The villagers were gathered outside in the dusk when Wilson was taken out of the motel, his hands chained behind him. The villagers stirred toward the soldiers, and the pellet guns came up quickly.

Wilson stepped forward. "Go home," he said. "They will not do to me anything that I do not permit. There will be another doctor here to help you while I am gone. Go home. Do not resist the Emperor's soldiers."

The villagers parted. The soldiers put him into the wagon and sat on the benches on either side as the horses started the wagon along the cracked, old, four-lane highway to the city.

III

Once more the voice of the bailiff parted the fog that filled his mind. "All rise. District court, Judge Green presiding, is now in session."

The twelve good men and true—some of them women, to be truly accurate—were back in their oak jury box. The little balcony above the jury was crowded. Wilson had the feeling that it was balanced precariously on stilts and that it might topple forward at any moment. As Wilson's gaze drifted around the room, he saw that the benches beyond the railing to his left were filled as well. He looked until he saw the blond girl and smiled. The television cameras were back, too, their red lights switching back and forth hypnotically.

Perhaps it was because he had been here before, perhaps, if it was true that he was drugged, that his tolerance for the drug was increasing, or perhaps, if this were a dream, that his subconscious was dredging up more detail to satisfy his conscious mind. Everything moved with elephantine slowness, and even in that slow progression there were curious gaps.

Perhaps the summer day was more humid and the old air conditioners in the back windows could not keep up; they chuffed continuously, but the arms of his chair had a slick, moist feel to them. The room smelled oddly—acrid and musky with human sweat from the bodies packed closely together, a little musty like decaying wood, and over it all the bite of burning incense.

Events had moved along in the courtroom, Wilson became aware. He had the impression that witnesses had been sitting in the chair to the right of the judge's bench and that they had been talking about him and a fire.

A university had been burned—not just a building or two but the entire fifty or so and now on top of the hill where once red roofs had been glimpsed from afar could be seen only black ruins. A janitor who had worked at the university testified, under the insistent questioning of the district attorney, that there had been late meetings in the offices he cleaned. He had overheard talk about setting fires, and he had retrieved from wastebaskets rough plans of the university buildings on which had been written the words "gasoline" or "thermite." The district attorney offered the sketches in evidence.

Youngman objected occasionally. Usually he was overruled. He asked to have the identification of the handwriting verified by an independent expert and was refused.

The dark-haired young man beside the district attorney who looked familiar to Wilson, in a dreamlike way, said nothing. Sometimes he smiled at Wilson. Occasionally he leaned over to whisper to the district attorney or to motion with his head at the cameras, and then the district attorney would ask the witness a question or make a motion to the judge.

Then there was a student on the stand who said something about discussions in class concerning the ignorance of the common man and how easily he was misled. He had reported the discussions to the local committee on academic practices. He also had made tape recordings of the discussion and of the teacher's lectures. He had recorded talk in class about the university burnings, too, and whether they would turn the people against the Senate Subcommittee on Academic Practices and, indeed, the whole Lowbrow movement.

It all was vaguely familiar, like an old dream, and about as important. Wilson gazed idly around the room again. Four old light fixtures hung from the tall ceiling. Some of the ceiling tiles were sagging. The air conditioners were thin, old, window units placed high in four tall windows at the back of the room, behind the cameras.

Suddenly he could not see as well. The room had darkened. Films were being shown at the front of the room. The scene was in a classroom, and mostly the films showed a single person, the teacher, at the head of the room. He should know the teacher, Wilson thought. Of course, it was himself. He felt good to realize that he had a piece of himself back; he had been a teacher. He had not been particularly good at it, though.

He looked rather ridiculous up there talking about things like the sociological significance of protest and the psychological content of lynching, about the values of the Lowbrow movement and the hypocrisy of Senator Bartlett and his Subcommittee, about the importance of the scientific method and the necessity for the detachment of the scientist.

The film was dull, and the lecture was dull and pointlessly pontifical, saying nothing repetitively. Wilson felt Youngman's elbow glance into his ribs and heard the lawyer mutter something. He nodded and stared past the screen at the front of the room. There were two doors, one on either side of the judge's bench. The one on the judge's right had a frosted window; in the other the glass was clear. The judge had come through the door on his right; the recorder, who was in charge of a complicated device just in front of the bench, had come through the door with the clear glass.

Wilson turned farther to his right. Behind him, Wilson was fascinated to discover, was another group of chairs —about a dozen, similar to those on the opposite side of the room for the jury. Only this side had no wooden back or platform to raise the second row of chairs. People were sitting in the chairs. They were dressed in ragged suits, most of them, with blue open-collared shirts beneath their coats. One face in particular drew Wilson's gaze. It was a face a little like that of an Old Testament prophet with a boyish, unruly mop of hair and eyes that looked at Wilson as if he were an object. Wilson looked at the man for a long time before the man looked away. Wilson decided that he knew the man, but he could not remember where.

Above the heads of the people sitting behind him were a group of large pictures hung in two rows on the wall. They were in oak frames of assorted sizes. Four of the men pictured in them had beards; three of the other four had mustaches.

That made it seven to one in favor of face hair, Wilson thought. He felt his chin. He was clean shaven. He did not remember shaving.

When he turned his gaze back to the front of the room, the films were more exciting. They were color films of a great fire. Buildings were burning, big ones with pillars and towers, built of stone and brick. Some of them were ruins of rubble and glowing coals, others were melting islands in a sea of flame.

If one looked closely one could see, as Wilson saw, black, stick figures running in front of the flames, back and forth, back and forth, until the realization came that they were not in front of the flames but in them, and they were consumed. It was the old nightmare. Wilson remembered it now with all its horror.

He moaned. "Sylvia!" he said beneath his breath. "Sammy!" The fog lifted a little from his brain and allowed the pain to lance through. Even as he watched the terrible scenes he remembered so well, he knew there was something he should do, something he had forgotten to do, something he must remember to do.

Then there was a face on the screen, a face painted with scarlet fingers, a face satanic in expression, a face trying to hide, it seemed, behind an unbuttoned shirt collar and a coat collar turned up. It was another familiar face. He knew that face. It was his own.

It was the face of guilt. He shrank from it. He turned his head away from it and met the gaze of Youngman at his side. Youngman's eyes were on him, asking him to do something, but Wilson's head was too filled with pain. Across from him the dark young man was looking at him, too, his lips curled in a mockery of a smile, his face changed by the scarlet reflections from the screen into a kind of devil's mask, not unlike Wilson's face there in the film. Behind him, Wilson had the feeling, other eyes were staring at the back of his head.

He stood up, swaying on his feet, and put his hand to his throat. He felt as if he were choking. There was a tie there, although he didn't remember putting on a tie. He felt his shoulders. He wore a coat. He ran his fingers tremblingly along the lapels. Suddenly he jerked them away with an exclamation of pain.

As the lights went up in the courtroom, he was standing at the table, looking down at his hand. There was blood on his right hand and more blood welling from a cut on his right index finger. Youngman reached out his handkerchief to staunch the flow of blood and got some on the sleeve of his coat.

The television cameras were staring at him. Wilson looked guiltily into their lenses.

IV

The room was on the third floor of a twenty-eight-story building located in the heart of the old city. It was on the third floor because the elevators had stopped working long ago and there was no point in climbing when so many comparable rooms were available elsewhere.

The city was thinly populated now, supported only by the desultory activities of the Emperor and his authorities. Those activities had to be located where the old highway systems focused, where river traffic was possible, and where an occasional steam-powered locomotive could tug in a string of decrepit cars on the rusty rails.

The room was large, but a corroded metal counter divided it in half. Wilson stood on the window side of the counter, where only a battered desk and a few rickety chairs cluttered the marble floors. The walls, too, were faced with marble higher than his head. A pot-bellied iron stove stood near a window where its black chimney pipe could snake through the shattered glass patched with plywood scavenged from somewhere else. The stove was cold now in the heat of the summer, but the room was cool.

The dark young man sat behind the desk, watching him. Wilson stood in front of the desk, waiting, his hands still chained behind him.

"So," the young man said finally, "you are a witch."

"That is what people call me."

"But you are not a witch."

"I am many things. To people who call me a witch, I am a witch. I have strange powers with which to control the natural world. I can do things that others cannot do, things they cannot even understand. For this they respect me; for my services in their behalf they sometimes pay me. I am their mediator between the goodness of life that they want and the evil in life that keeps them from having it."

"You are an educated man who uses the old science to

delude the people. The Emperor wants to know where you got your learning, and he wants to know where you got your building and equipment and how it is defended and where you get your supplies."

"The Emperor wants to know a great deal. That is the beginning of education."

"It is not wise to joke about the Emperor," the young man said.

"I do not joke," Wilson said.

"The Emperor does not want education," the young man snapped. "He wants information. He will get it from you." He settled back in his chair. "You have succeeded in stirring me once against my will. If you succeed again you will be a clever man, too clever to be allowed to exist. We will be put to the trouble of finding another witch."

"I would not willingly trouble anyone."

"You would be wise especially not to trouble the head of the Emperor's secret police."

"You are young for such eminence."

The young man smiled. "There is no age requirement for competence."

"Nor for ambition. And what is this competent young man's name?"

"You may call me 'Captain.' "

"You do think of me as a witch, Captain."

"Why do you say that?"

"You do not give me your name. Is it because, after all, you believe that if I know your name I might have power over you?"

"Peasant superstition."

"And yet—?"

"You will not taunt me into revealing my name to you. I think you have no power, and yet who knows what power the old science may give you? A prudent man— But you are clever! I have brought you here to answer my questions, and you have me answering yours. In the end it will avail you nothing, however; you will answer my questions."

"And then?"

"If you are cooperative the Emperor may choose to be merciful."

"The Emperor's mercy is well known. But I am a man who lives by reason. If I cooperate I will need to be convinced that my cooperation is merited. You will have to answer my questions."

"Ask your questions," the young man said, shrugging.

"Why does the Emperor suddenly interest himself in the villages?"

"The Emperor is interested in every part of his empire, now and always."

"But he has not interfered in the internal affairs of the villages for a decade. That was when the last witch-hunt ended in failure."

"So I have heard. But this is not a witch-hunt. What is one witch more or less?"

Wilson stood squarely in front of the young man, not shifting his weight, his shoulders pulled back by the chains binding his wrists. "Don't the villagers pay their taxes?"

"Only when soldiers are sent for them, and even then there is not much. A few trinkets but no coins, and grain and livestock are too bulky for soldiers to carry."

"The villagers have little need for money."

"Thanks to you and your fellow witches. They have only to ask for help and you give it to them. How can they develop their initiative, their ability to help themselves?"

"And yet we keep the villages peaceful, the villagers happy. Surely the Emperor counts this a blessing. There have been no uprisings."

"How can sheep rebel? We are an annoyance to them; we should be indispensable."

"As are their witches," Wilson said simply. "The Emperor begrudges us that."

"The Emperor begrudges nothing. He rules an empire stretching from St. Louis to Denver. It is the largest and greatest empire in the world, but it is only a shadow of what it might be. You and your fellow witches keep it feeble. Instead of sturdy, ambitious subjects, he has villages of listless farmers. Instead of a bustling empire filled with the sound of factories turning out goods for export, he has a land that is content to listen to the corn growing. How long before such a nation is conquered by its neighbors?"

"What difference would it make to the villagers?"

"It would make a difference to the Emperor. And it would make a difference to the villagers if they had the ambition to improve their lots, to produce for trade instead of consumption, to move their excess populations to the cities where they can put the factories to work again, revive the mines, repair the refineries, get the economy going. . . ."

"Back to the machines?" Wilson shook his head. "Your Emperor's predecessors did their job too well. A hatred of machines is bred into the people. They cannot go back."

"You give them machines."

"Those are not machines. They are magic, and the people are not tied to them. They are to serve, not to be served."

"The people won't go back as long as you and your fellow witches give them the benefits of the machine without responsibility for it. The Emperor calls you the opiate of the people."

Wilson smiled.

The young man's eyes smoldered. "It is you witches who oppress the people. Once relieved of your crutch they will find that they never needed you. They will have to return to the cities; they will have to return to progress."

Wilson chuckled.

"You laugh?" the young man asked incredulously.

"At the irony. First you destroy science and the machines science built, and then you struggle to get them back. It is all a matter of leverage for those who wield power—or want to."

"There would be no struggle if it were not for you. Our Emperor has the interests of the people in his heart; he wants to see them happy and prospering. He does not want them ground under the heel of a conqueror."

"Does someone threaten war?" Wilson asked. "That is hard to believe. Conditions are much the same everywhere—only a few young men who cannot master the teachings or the way of life of the villages or who grow up untutored in the city's ruins become soldiers. There are too few to fight a war of conquest; there is not enough transportation or enough material. But perhaps it is the Emperor who grows restless. Would he like to expand his empire? Is it he who plans a war of conquest?"

The young man looked at Wilson with hard eyes and unmoving face. "Enough of your questions. Now you will answer mine."

"Ask."

"Where did you get your knowledge?"

"I was educated in a village not far from here."

"You did not learn all you know in a village school," the young man said sharply. "We have questioned villagers, and they have an interesting amount of misinformation and information of little value to them or anyone else, but they are filled with superstition and they do not know how to heal the sick or how to make the land fertile or how to repair their machines when they stop working."

"When I was a young man," Wilson said, his eyes reminiscent, "there still were universities. I learned many things in one of them but more in the villages. I traveled from village to village working, talking to the people, learning from them. Eventually, by contemplation and perseverance, I found my way to truth."

"What is truth?"

"You will pardon me, Captain," Wilson said, as he moved slowly toward the unbroken window pane that was left and looked out into the street three floors below. It was cluttered with debris from the building opposite, which had been burned long before, and with rusted vehicles of various kinds, now little more than mounds of ore. A path wide enough for a wagon had been created in the center of the old street. Otherwise the street was the way it had been left when the city was abandoned by all except the scavengers. The street was empty and silent.

"If I could tell you what I found," Wilson said, turning back to the young man at the desk, "I would not have had to go to seek it. No one could tell me. At best I could only be prepared to find it and to know it when I found it and was ready to accept it. What is truth? I cannot tell you, Captain. I can only tell you where to find it."

"Where will I find it?"

"Among the people and in your heart and mind. It is the secret of the people's survival and their fitness to survive. It is what the people must be to survive and how they must be selected if they are to evolve."

"All this is the superstition you feed the villagers to keep them under your spell," the young man said impatiently. "What is it you found? Where did you get your knowledge?"

"This is not something you can pass along like a multiplication table, Captain. You must find it for yourself, with humility and an open mind."

"Rubbish! Where do you get your buildings? Where do you get your supplies?"

"From those who also have found truth."

The young man sat in his chair looking at Wilson. "You will tell me these things," he said at last. "We have some of the old drugs that are reputed to loosen tongues, and if these have lost their powers we can try methods more physical. And when you have told us all we wish to know, you will go on trial as a witch."

"How will you try me," Wilson asked, "when you already have judged me?"

"Sergeant," the young man called out. The leader of the platoon came through the doorway followed by two of his soldiers.

The young man smiled. "By fire, witch. How else?"

V

A woman was sitting in the witness chair when the courtroom swam back into Wilson's consciousness. Except for her the room was just as it had been before—the jury, the two men at the table opposite, Youngman beside him, the stone-faced audience, the peering eyes of the television cameras, the men sitting behind him under the pictures of the eight old men, seven of them with beards or mustaches.

It had the recurring quality of a nightmare, but it moved along. Which was real? he wondered fuzzily. Was he the witch-doctor in a world of villages being put to the question and dreaming of a world in which science was being repudiated? Or was he a scientist on trial for burning a university and dreaming of a world in which the scientist was a respected and beloved helper of the people?

He could not decide. He knew, though, which one he hoped was real—and this was not it.

There were so many things he did not know. He did not know whether he was guilty, as this vaguely familiar woman in the chair seemed to be saying. The lawyer who was defending him—he had said Wilson was not guilty. But that was what lawyers always said, wasn't it? Or else there would be few trials.

The district attorney was asking the woman questions about the evening the university had burned. "You saw the defendant that evening, Mrs. Craddock?"

"He was at our house. We had dinner, and he said—"

"Who is this man? Can you identify him for us, Mrs. Craddock?"

"John Wilson," Mrs. Craddock said. "That man sitting there," she said, pointing.

She was an attractive woman, Wilson thought, but an unattractive emotion was distorting her features. Was it hatred?

"The defendant?"

"Yes. He said Harvard had burned and Cal Tech had burned, and the University would be next."

"And by 'the University' he meant—?"

"We all knew what he meant. The university he worked for."

"And why did he think the University would be next?"

"He didn't say, but he gave us the impression that it was inevitable. That it was already determined."

"That it was planned?"

"Yes."

"That it would be soon?"

"Yes."

"And did you get the impression from the defendant that he had been part of the planning?"

"Yes—"

Youngman objected, and the judge ordered it stricken from the record, but the audience had heard it—and it stirred them to an animal moan. The television viewers had heard it. And most of all the jurors had heard it. They were ready to declare him guilty on the spot, Wilson felt. As a matter of fact, he was ready to admit his own guilt. If he could only remember! But his mind was filled with swirling fog.

He half rose in his chair. "Emily?" he began. "Emily—?" And he could not continue, because the thought had come to him that the name of the woman on the witness stand was "Emily," and he had remembered that much. And he could remember vaguely an evening when he had eaten at a table with Emily and someone named Mark and two children named Amy and Junior, and he had said something like the things that Emily had said. Only it was not quite right.

He stood there in front of the jury and the audience and the television eyes, and it was like an admission of guilt that he should speak the woman's name but say no more but he could not think of what else to say but "Emily." The woman he knew by that name frowned and unconsciously bit her lower lip. The dark young man who sat at the table opposite him and had not yet spoken aloud braced his hands upon his chair as if he were about to rise.

"Sit down, Mr. Wilson!" the judge ordered. "You may not interrupt the trial. If you wish to be heard, you must appear as a witness."

Youngman's hand touched Wilson's arm, and Wilson sank back to his seat, bemused.

After Youngman's cross-examination, unshaken but with apparent relief, Mrs. Craddock was allowed to leave the witness chair. She was followed to the chair by others. A man identified as a desk clerk at a downtown hotel testified that on the night of the fire he had seen the defendant get off a bus from this town, make a telephone call, and then register at the hotel under the name of "Gerald Perry" and with the occupation of "salesman from Rochester, N.Y." He had left in the middle of the night. No one had seen him go.

A seedy middle-aged man said that he had been paid by Wilson to pick up a package addressed to Wilson at general delivery and then to toss it behind a bush as he left the post office. Immediately afterward he had been accosted by detectives who were hunting for Wilson but by the time they had returned to the spot Wilson had fled.

An old man testified that a man who looked like Wilson had bought a hearing aid from him for $239.95 on the day following the fire, and a young man, who had clerked at that time in an electronics parts store, said that on the day following the fire Wilson had paid him $153 for parts and the use of a workroom and tools.

A broad-shouldered, thick-necked man with a nose that had been broken sometime in the recent past identified

himself as an investigator for the Senate Subcommittee on
Academic Practices and testified that he had picked up
Wilson in New Orleans as Wilson was about to sell his
services to an agent for the government of Brazil, along
with whatever secrets he had in his possession.

Youngman objected again. "What is the relevance of
the testimony of these witnesses to the crime of which my
client is accused? These actions are readily interpreted as
those of a man in great fear of his personal safety, as
who would not be if he had seen his university burned
and his friends slain by a mob? I ask that all this testimony be struck from the record and that the jury be
asked to disregard it."

The judge looked at the district attorney, and the
blocky man turned to the dark young man beside him.
The young man whispered in the district attorney's ear,
his hand cupped in front of his mouth.

"Your honor," said the district attorney, rising to his
feet, "I am shocked at the attorney for the defense accus-
ing the people of this state and of this nation of mob
actions. I would remind the court and the attorney that
they are not on trial. The witnesses who have appeared
before this court have painted a picture of a man whose
actions are not those of an innocent person who had only
to enter the nearest police station if he needed protection. He could there have entered a complaint against
others if he felt they were responsible for this tragic
event. Instead he assumed a false name, persuaded others
to act for him under suspicious circumstances, obtained
devices for which he had no legal use, and attempted to
slip illegally out of the country. These are the actions of
a man ridden with guilt and trying to evade the natural
consequences of his actions—"

"Your honor," Youngman said, half-rising, "the district
attorney is making a speech."

"All the testimony given today is pertinent, your hon-
or," the district attorney said. "And it will lead to other
revelations."

"Will it lead to the revelation," Youngman asked, "that
I have not been permitted to consult with my client since
his arrest, an official action which prejudices the entire
trial and which will be called to the attention of the
appellate court as soon as this trial is concluded?"

"Are you raising an objection, Mr. Youngman?" the judge asked evenly.

"I am objecting to the entire nature and structure of this trial," Youngman said clearly. "It is a farce to think that this man can defend himself without consultation. This man has not even been allowed to see his wife since his imprisonment. If this state of affairs continues, if my client is prevented from communicating with his lawyer and his family, I will refuse to let my client take the stand, and we will appeal this case to the highest court."

The jury stirred. The audience groaned. A blond young woman stood up in the audience and screamed. Then, putting the back of her hand to her lips, she crumpled to the floor.

How fascinating, Wilson thought. Was that woman his wife? She looked familiar all right. He had seen her before. She looked like the Pat Helman of his dream—or his dream of the Pat Helman of his real existence.

VI

Wilson's senses were numb, but the very numbness seemed to enhance his subconscious awareness. He had, for instance, a feeling that he was in a building of immense size. The room itself was relatively small. The walls were stone, and a stone fireplace with a marble mantel was built into the far wall. Several old tubular metal chairs with leatherette upholstery were placed neatly against the walls. A single tall window broke the wall at his right; it was latticed with metal bars. A thick doorway was to his left. Beyond it were two uniformed guards, and beyond them was a peering lens mounted on a tripod. It made a muted, whirring noise.

Besides the feeling of massive size, Wilson also sensed a strong institutional odor of soap and antiseptic. In addition he sensed, nearer, a more subtle fragrance that he had not smelled for a long time, for many months, but it brought back memories of a girl driving a long Cadillac Turbo-jet 500, a girl with bright golden hair like a scarf tugging at her head, with blue eyes and warm lips and a throat like a white column.

He was not surprised that she was sitting beside him, but then little seemed to surprise him. "You've—you've cut—your hair," he got out. Her hair was straight and short now, not much longer than a man's, with soft bangs across her forehead, but she was as lovely as ever. She dressed more sedately, too, than his errant memory recalled.

"Yes, darling," she said. "I'm an old married lady now." She held out a left hand with a thick gold ring on it.

"Married?" he echoed.

"Oh, what have they done to you?" she wailed. And she threw herself at him. Her arms went around his neck. Her head buried itself in the hollow between his neck and his shoulder, and he felt something sting the back of his neck. "To you, John Wilson," she whispered in his ear. He straightened and for a moment the clouds in his head parted. "I'm sorry," she said an instant later as she pulled herself away and rearranged her hair. "I lost control of myself. I promised myself I wouldn't do that. You have enough to worry about without that."

He looked at her, trying to remember. Her name was Pat Helman—maybe—or perhaps it was Pat Wilson, Mrs. John Wilson. But surely he would be more certain about his wife. He was on trial for something to do with the burning of a university. He remembered that. And now he must be in prison where he was being visited by this woman who said she was his wife.

She had been talking for several minutes and he had not been listening, he realized guiltily. He tried to concentrate on what she was saying.

"You must try to understand, Johnny. They let one of us visit you. Only one. It's just for show, of course, but Charley and I—that's Charley Youngman, your lawyer— decided that we couldn't pass up the opportunity. We talked it over and decided I should come, that maybe I could get through to you better.

"You're on trial for your life, Johnny. They'll hang you for sure if you don't do something. As payment for this visit we've agreed to let you take the witness stand in your own defense, but you've got to snap out of it or they'll cut you up."

The fog was beginning to drift away, he thought, and

a moment later he was sure of it. First came the stab of remembrance like a flaming sword, and the flames spread until they ate away a great and beautiful university and then consumed its beating heart, the men and women who taught and studied there, friends of his, colleagues, and one who was more than a friend. The pain made his eyes lower to his hands where they rested motionless on his legs like paralyzed white spiders.

"You're not guilty, Johnny," the blond girl was saying, "but you're acting as if you were. And that's the same thing."

No, he wasn't guilty. He remembered now the way it was. When he was a boy he and some friends had fired an old grain bin to kill the rats as they came out. That's the way it had been that night.

"The time is almost up," the girl said. "They've given us only half an hour. You're going to be all right. I know it, now."

Yes, he was going to be all right if he could only keep remembering and not forget. He could remember the terror and desperation of the long escape to New Orleans. They had traced his every step, these people who were trying him for the crimes of all scientists. The only facts they did not have—or at least that they had not revealed yet—were this girl beside him, who was not, he thought regretfully, Mrs. Wilson, and the shadowy organization she represented.

She had picked him up on the highway after he had left the train at Alexandria and his second-hand car had given up. "I'm old Tim Helman's only child," she had said, "and I have a guilt complex a runway long." He knew who Tim Helman was—he was the financier who had put his money and the money of millions of others into commercial rocketports and artificial satellites. He was the man who had lost it all when the Lowbrow movement came along and the government revoked his subsidies before the complex could start paying off. He was the man who had died of a heart attack—it was announced as a heart attack—before he could be brought to trial for fraud under a blue-sky law that was, for once, aptly named.

Later, Pat Helman and a man named Pike had convinced him that he and his fellow scientists were as blindly wrong in their pursuit of inhuman truth as the mobs who made up the Lowbrow movement were wrong in their massacre of the scientists. He had gone to live with the people, to see if he could become one of them instead of an egghead walled off by an impenetrable shell of superiority, to determine if he could learn from them what they were trying to communicate by violence.

Now Wilson understood these matters emotionally as well as intellectually, and he thought he understood the people. He understood their need for a scapegoat to take the blame for their sins, and he also understood their desires for someone better than themselves to represent their finest aspirations. He had given himself up as one or the other. What was it to be?

"Oh, Johnny," said Pat Helman, whose name was not Wilson and never had been and perhaps never would be. "It's all up to you. I've got to go now. I may never see you again." Once more she threw herself at him, and again she whispered against his ear. "We didn't mean for you to give yourself up, you idiot! We can't get you out of here or that courtroom either. All we can do is give you the antidote to the drugs, which I've done. You mustn't let on though, or they'll never put you on the stand, and your martyrdom might as well pay off in one moment of glory." And then she pulled herself away. "Good-by, Johnny. Good-by."

He was left alone in the little room, staring after her, staring into the eye of the camera which had recorded this touching moment of reunion between a notorious criminal and his wife, through official generosity, and he dulled his eyes and let them sink to his hands as the guards came and led him unresisting down the echoing corridors to his cell.

VII

The words in the relentless whisper echoed in his ears, "You are a witch, a witch, a witch. Where do you get your wit, your wit, your wit?" The echo was inside his head, which was a great empty space.

He opened his eyes and saw nothing. At first he thought that he was blind and then, as a shadow pirouetted across the ceiling, he realized that the cell was lit by a single candle in the corner. He could not summon the will to look at it but he knew it was there by the shadows.

He was lying on crumbling cement. He could feel it dusty beneath his hands. From the musty smell of the place it might be an underground room, perhaps a room in the same old City Hall in which he had talked with the young man who called himself Captain.

"Who are you? What is your name?" came the whisper again.

"John Wilson," he said with difficulty but with precision. He did not need to look. The dark young man was seated on the cement beside him.

"John Wilson," the young man said, "you will tell me what I need to know."

"I will tell you—what you need to know," Wilson repeated. The words were the same but the meaning somehow was different.

The young man felt it, too. "You will tell me what I wish to know."

"I will tell you—what you need to know," Wilson said.

"Where did you get your education?" came the whisper.

"Part of it—before the destruction—of the machines."

"But that would make you more than one hundred years old!" the young man snapped. Wilson did not say anything. It was not a question. "Are you more than one hundred years old?"

"Yes."

"That's ridiculous! You do not look more than middle aged." Again there was silence. "How can such things be?"

"Much is possible—for men who have found truth," Wilson got up. "Disease is unnecessary. Aging can be delayed."

The young man was silent again. Perhaps he was absorbing the implications of the information he had received. What would the Emperor give for the secret of longevity? What could the young man himself do with another half century or more of vigorous life in which to get ahead in the world? It might change his entire outlook upon his career; he might not have to take shortcuts to win success while he still could enjoy its fruits.

The silence endured until Wilson was afraid he would fall back into the cavern inside his head. But he clung to consciousness as if it were the edge of a cliff. Next time he might not have so firm a grip on his cavern—on his mind.

"Are you telling the truth?"

"Can I tell—anything else?"

"Always you answer a question with a question. Why?"

"That is the nature of man—and the nature of life. There are no final answers—only new questions."

"Mysticism! The answers I want are not so difficult. Where did you get the rest of your education?"

"Everywhere."

"Are you a witch?"

"To some."

"Where are your fellow witches?"

"In the villages."

"Where do they get their support?"

"From the villages."

"They do not get their machines from the villages nor their supplies. Where is the witch world? Where is the place that witches learn their craft? Where do they get their machines?"

"The witch world—co-exists with the empire—and with all other kingdoms and empires of the world."

"Where else is it?"

"Wherever man can exist."

"And where is that?"

"Everywhere."

"You are evading my questions. Have you the will to do that?"

"The will—and the capability."

"Then there are other methods of persuasion."

Distantly Wilson felt his hand lifted. The shadows swirled on the ceiling above his head. He did not feel pain, but in a few moments the odor of cooking meat drifted to his nostrils.

"A foretaste of the flames," the young man said.

"Your measures combat each other," Wilson said. "I feel nothing. Burn away. Or if you would have me suffer —you must give me the power—to resist."

"You devil!" As distantly as it was lifted, Wilson felt

his hand dropped, and the shadows danced once more across the ceiling. "Why did you let yourself be captured?"

"If not me then another."

"The villagers could have resisted. They could have overcome us."

"They are peaceful folk. Violence breeds more violence. Other soldiers would come. So long as the Emperor is content—to rule the body without coercing the spirit—the Empire will exist and the people will obey it. The life the people have—is beyond the realm of the Emperor."

"You are speaking nonsense again," the young man said, but he said it absently. "Would you like your right hand to match your left? Let me tell you what the Emperor has in mind. If the witches would support him with goods and machines—and you have them, we know—he could soon conquer this entire continent, eventually perhaps the world itself. All the world under one peaceful rule. Think of that! And you witches would be well repaid."

"Sometime in his life every ruler has that dream," Wilson said. "The answer is always the same. You cannot give us anything we do not already have. You can only take from the people."

"You are an obstinate and short-sighted witch!"

Wilson summoned his energies once more. "You are an inquisitive young man. You wish to know. If you had attended a village school—you would know much already."

"I attended the Court School. And I learned much there but even more at the Court itself. You see where it has taken me."

"From ignorance to ignorance," Wilson said. "It is not too late. I was ten years older than you are before my education truly began. You still can learn. Go seek the truth. What distinguishes half-man from animal? What separates man from half-man? What will select next man from present man?"

"What should I care about such follies? Be still, old man."

"You may be next man. But you must find your way. You must pass the tests. To be fit to survive you must survive."

"You talk rubbish, old man," the young man said,

but he sounded uneasy. He was thoughtful for a few moments and then, Wilson thought, he shook himself like a dog coming out of a cold bath. "Next man or past man, you will burn, old man. We will put you to the trial, and then you will be dead man."

"You do not fear the witch's power?"

"Let it save you from the flames. Perhaps then I will believe in witchcraft and your mumbo-jumbo."

"Then it may be too late. The man who can be convinced only by a show of force—is lost to reason."

"Reason is a weak man's solace."

"Force is a strong man's refuge."

"You will burn brightly!"

"Burn me brightly then," Wilson said. "Perhaps by my light you may see a part of the truth. You will not have another chance. I am the only witch we will allow the Emperor to take." And Wilson loosened his grasp upon the cliff of consciousness and fell back into the cavern and dreamed of flames.

VIII

Wilson woke not to the dim confusion of the courtroom but to the pale light of morning filtering through tall windows lined with bars. His pillow was whispering to him, "You are a witch, and you have set a fire—a fire which destroyed a university and the people in it, people who were your friends and now are dead ashes. You are guilty. You have committed arson and murder, and you must be punished."

More bars were all around him—bars for walls, bars for a door. Only above him and below him was there something solid—the ceiling and the floor were concrete, but Wilson felt that inside them, if he dug, he would find the same cold, gray bars.

He was in a cell. It was part of a block of cells stacked one atop and beside another like so many houses built of toothpicks, but the toothpicks were solid steel. Outside his cell was a corridor and beyond that was a stone wall. The tall, barred windows were in the wall. He was a prisoner held in a maximum security prison, and he had no more chance of escaping than a witch from the deepest Inquisitorial dungeon.

He ran his hand over the rough material of the prison blanket that covered him, and over the dustily astringent odor of mopped concrete floors he smelled coffee brewing far off. How long had it been since he had smelled something so good? They had taken that from him, and he lay in his bunk, listening to his pillow, and enjoyed the smell.

"You're awake, eh?" said an interested voice close beside him. "It's the first time you've been awake."

Wilson's eyes slowly drifted shut.

"Oh," the voice said, disappointed. "I guess you ain't. But if you are and don't want to let on, I want to talk to you when you get a chance to listen. They say you're a crummy scientist, but you don't seem so bad to me. You just lay there, moaning and talking in your sleep, and I guess you're just a crummy con like me, and it's us against them. We got something working, fellow, and if you want a piece of it just wiggle your eyelids."

Wilson lay very still, breathing regularly, listening to his vindictive pillow. His eyelids did not move.

"I don't blame you, fellow," said the voice beside him. "Why should you trust anybody? Maybe when they bring you back—if they bring you back."

They came soon afterwards. Men dressed Wilson's unresisting body in newly pressed clothes and half carried, half dragged him to an armored truck. It had two cots in the back, and they placed Wilson on one of them. The truck started up. After about ten minutes of slow, twisting city driving, the truck picked up speed. Twenty minutes later it drew up to the back of an old brick building. Wilson was hustled into a small doorway and up a flight of stairs to the courtroom.

"No one will appear in this man's defense," Youngman said. "His cause is unpopular, and anyone who testifies for him will be called 'traitor' by his neighbors, and perhaps worse will happen to him. Therefore I will call John Wilson himself to be the only witness for the defense."

With great care, as if he were walking a tightrope, Wilson made his way to the witness chair and with Youngman's aid settled himself into it. Slowly Youngman led him through a rebuttal of the testimony presented by the prosecution. Wilson hesitated often and fumbled for words, but he finally told his story of the events.

He had returned to find the University already in flames, he said. He had fled the scene and later the area under an assumed name for fear that what had happened to the others at the University would happen to him. By the time Youngman had finished, they had painted a picture of a man driven by desperation into a wild and sometimes irrational flight for his life.

Youngman turned to the district attorney and took his seat. The district attorney hesitated for a moment, frowning, looked at the young man seated beside him, and then pulled himself up.

"You claim that you returned to the University to find it in flames. And yet Mrs. Craddock points out that you were talking about plans to burn it at dinner that evening."

Wilson straightened a little. "Not plans," he said gently. "The possibility of others burning it. And by the testimony of your own witnesses, Mrs. Craddock and the officials who noted the time of the fire, I left the city after the fire already had begun 35 miles away."

The district attorney seemed unable to find an appropriate word. He turned halfway toward the young man sitting at the table. Smoothly the young man got up. "Your honor? May I interrogate the witness?"

The voice was familiar.

The judge nodded. "Of course, Mr. Kelley. You have been appointed assistant prosecutor for that purpose."

Now Wilson knew him. Leonard Kelley was chief investigator for Senator Bartlett's Subcommittee on Academic Practices.

"Mr. Wilson," Kelley said smoothly, "you are, as you know, not accused of setting the fire itself but of conspiring with others to set it. That you were not there to put the torch yourself is incidental, and you are only trying to confuse the jury by pretending otherwise. You will not deny that your actions following the fire were those of a guilty man."

"It is a truism that the guilty flee when no man pursueth," Wilson said drily, straightening a little more. "But it is equally true and equally obvious that the wise man, when he sees an angry mob approaching with a rope, does not stop to ask questions."

Kelley studied Wilson's face with shrewd, perceptive eyes. "You were trying to flee the country entirely when you were captured."

"A moment of folly. Luckily I thought better of it and returned."

"You mean you were returned."

"No, I returned of my own volition, having escaped from the agent of the Subcommittee."

"You escaped, Wilson? How?"

"Your colleague lost his head—and had his nose somewhat altered."

"And then what did you do, Wilson?"

"I returned. Three months later I gave myself up voluntarily."

The members of the jury turned to each other. The stern-faced members of the audience shifted positions.

"What did you do in those three months, Wilson?"

"I lived in small towns, worked in the fields and in the shops."

"Did you believe that this would enable you to escape justice?"

"I knew that I could avoid recapture," Wilson said with a careful choice of words, "but I was living in these places in this way so that I could learn why the people hate scientists."

Kelley turned toward the jury and the audience until his back was almost to Wilson. "I am glad that you admit this basic truth, Wilson. The people hate scientists, and they have good reason to hate. But why do you think they hate you, Wilson?"

"Not me personally," Wilson said. "All scientists. Blame for that lies on both sides—the scientists are at fault because they have been blind to the needs of the people for security, and the people, because they have been unable to see that the only security is death—or a way of life so like death that it is scarcely distinguishable."

"You are condemning the people to death?"

"You twist my words. The people must accept the fact of insecurity. I do not say it; life insists on it. The people must find their security in their own ability to cope with change. The scientist, on the other hand, must give up his childlike worship of science.

"One of the great philosophers of science, T. H. Huxley, summed it up this way, 'Science seems to me to teach in the highest and strongest manner the great truth which is embodied in the Christian conception of entire surrender to the will of God. Sit down before fact as a little child, be prepared to give up every pre-conceived notion, follow humbly wherever and to whatever abysses Nature leads, or you shall learn nothing.' The scientist must recognize that he still is a layman in every field but one, and in that one field he must accept the consequences of his actions, reckoning the human payment for every change and communicating broadly the information that is peculiarly his own. I do not say it; the gulf between the people and the scientists demands it."

"You claim that they are a separate breed, the people and the scientists?"

"Their attitudes set them apart; their common interests and their common heritage must bring them back together. The scientist is rational man at work; the mob is irrational, wherein lies the ultimate terror for the reasoning man."

"Now you are calling the people irrational!"

"Only when they act like a mob or when, like the scientist when he is out of his laboratory, they are sentimentalists. The sentimentalist is the person who wants to eat his cake and have it, too. G. K. Chesterton once said about him, 'He has no sense of honor about ideas; he will not see that one must pay for an idea as for anything else. He will have them all at once in one wild intellectual harem, no matter how much they quarrel and contradict each other.' "

Kelley studied the audience and the jury and then looked back at Wilson. "Science never has reckoned the consequences for any of its actions or computed the human payment that must be made. Why should it start now?"

"Men once never herded cattle or tilled the land or lived in cities or traveled in airplanes. Tribes once killed every stranger. Kings once cut off the heads of the bearers of ill tidings. Senators once were elected by state legislatures."

"Are you trying to tell us that men change?" Kelley asked.

"That is obvious to everyone except the cynic. Men can change and they do. This is not only a possibility for the individual and a necessity for society but a historical inevitability. Our perspective is too short for us to recognize the phenomenon in action, but men evolve. We can see it happening more swiftly in their social institutions."

"How do you think men are changing, Wilson?"

Wilson smiled. Kelley was willing to let him convict himself out of his own mouth, not only before the jury here in the courtroom but before the broader jury of the nation. But it was more important to Wilson that he get these concepts on the record, not just for now, important as it was, but for the years to come.

"Surpluses slow down the process of change," Wilson said. "Shortages speed it up. Necessity is not only the mother of invention but of evolution. Surpluses are created by advancing stages of civilization, and population expands to consume them. When primitive man progressed from nut and fruit gathering to the hunting of concentrated sources of protein on the hoof, he had extra food with which he could feed the child which once might have been sacrificed to starvation.

"When the hunter became the farmer and the herder, the process of selection became slowed even more. He could nurse the sick as well as feeding the unable and the unwilling. The coming of the machine and industrialization brought further surpluses and the further development of morality and ethics and the religions that glorify weakness. Evolution is further slowed."

"Are you now attacking the Christian religion?" Kelley asked sharply.

Wilson waited until the roar of the audience died away. "Other religions do the same thing." The roar returned. "Moreover, I am a Christian—though, to be sure, a Unitarian. Christianity is one of the finest ethical and moral philosophies man ever has conceived, but it is a philosophy bred of surpluses. It could never have been possible to a tribe living on the narrow edge of starvation.

"The concern of that tribe is for the traits that will promote survival in this life, not in the next. That tribe's religious rites are basically evolutionary. When man was recently separated from his apelike ancestors, many throwbacks must have been born. They had to be weeded out."

"How, Wilson?"

Again Kelley was leading him, Wilson thought. Let him lead as long as the ideas came out. "The rite of manhood was the principal method—not merely adulthood but manhood. As soon as the child was old enough to have reached discretion, he was subjected to some ritualistic torture or feat of endurance. Scars were scratched into his body and face, lips and earlobes were distended by progressively larger plugs, food was withheld or voluntarily abjured. This was true of the American Indian and even in some of the countries considered more civilized it was part of the rites preceding knighthood.

"All of these rites stressed a common element—present sacrifice for future good, something no animal can comprehend, something only the human can consciously achieve. Imagine a tribal meeting around a campfire. The adolescent stands straight before the fire, hoping he can endure what lies ahead, anticipating the joys of manhood if he can come through without disgrace. The chief or the witch doctor picks up a burning brand from the fire and hands it to the boy, flames toward him. If the boy is human he accepts it, lets it burn him to prove that he is fit to join the adults of the tribe. If he is animal, if he is not fit, he refuses to take it or lets it drop—and he is killed, or he is killed genetically by the refusal of any young woman of the tribe to mate with him."

"Are you suggesting," Kelley asked, "that the American people return to that kind of tribal rite?"

"The time when that would have been effective has passed. We have other tribal rites, only they are not as effective in producing the desired results. The greatest examples of present sacrifice for future good are found in religions, and its greatest symbol is Christ on the Cross. Today we need a new device, a new evolutionary pressure, or a new rite to select the men and women who are capable of living in close association with the machine."

"Why should we wish to do that?" Kelley asked. "Why not merely destroy the machines and return to a better life?"

"Some always want to go back," Wilson said patiently. "Serfs who cannot accept industrialization, hunters who constitutionally cannot tie themselves to a single plot of ground, nut gatherers who can't eat meat, animals who will not suffer now to live better later. But you can't go back. At least you can't go back as you are. You go back decimated. This world cannot support more than a few hundred million people by primitive agriculture alone. If you discard the machines, four billion of you out there will die."

The jury came upright in its chairs. The audience looked startled, and men and women turned to one another to murmur. Kelley jerked his head squarely enough to talk to Wilson. "Scare talk! That's the kind of unprovable predictions with which scientists have always tried to get what they want. You can't trust a scientist. We've found that out."

"There is enough evidence to prove everything I have said," Wilson said, "but proof really is unnecessary. Simple logic will tell you that I am right. Simple logic will tell you, too, that man is perfectible. He can go on to greater works, greater glories, greater humanity. In every one of you," Wilson said, turning to the jury and then to the audience and the cameras, "is that potential. The only requirement is the willingness to live with change, with insecurity—the willingness to accept the burning brand, to let yourself be nailed to the cross of your own convictions. This thought, and the hope of getting it across, was the real reason I gave myself up."

"Are you comparing yourself to Christ?" Kelley snapped.

"God help me," Wilson said, "I hope not."

Kelley hesitated and then turned to the judge. "Your honor, I request that this session be adjourned and that this cross-examination be continued tomorrow."

Youngman was on his feet much quicker than Wilson ever had seen him move before. "Your honor, I see no grounds for this unusual request. The session is scarcely an hour old. If the assistant prosecutor wishes to conclude his cross-examination, we will consent. If not, I ask that he be instructed to continue."

"The witness has been questioned for a considerable time," Kelley said smoothly. "My request was only out of consideration for him."

"I feel fine," Wilson said. He glanced at Youngman. The lawyer nodded encouragingly. "Tomorrow, when the

Subcommittee's doctors get through with me, I may not feel so well."

The judge looked from Youngman to Kelley to Wilson, his lips pursed. He glanced quickly to his left and said, "Continue your examination, Counselor."

"Wilson," Kelley said without hesitation, "you have called for a new selection process by which men will be chosen for this new world of yours. Are these to be supermen—like you?"

"Like me, perhaps," Wilson said quietly. "I have enough vanity to think that I might be qualified to live in a changing world, to adapt to its demands, and to pass along my talents to children that someday I might have. But no more superman than the farmer was a superman to the hunter or the mechanic to the farmer."

"And where will these supermen be selected," Kelley asked, sneering, "in the universities?"

Kelley had not been corrected, and Wilson supposed he never would be. No matter what anyone said, the concept would stick. "Some were for awhile. College graduates, on the whole, were more successful in their society. They made more money, accumulated more authority, and sometimes passed along their traits and their power to their children, who also went to college. A greater proportion of the population was going on to higher education; they were becoming a majority, which might have meant a new plateau of selectivity, but, unfortunately, higher education wasn't adaptable to everybody's needs. More important, it was not responsive to the needs of the future, and somewhat lacking in the needs of the present. The universities became isolated from society, intellectually inbred, and the things for which they were selecting their students were idle intellectual pastimes not correlating well with success in the world outside."

"I had not expected you to provide the justification for the burning of the universities by the people," Kelley said. "You know, of course, that the nation's tax-free colleges and universities and the tax-free philanthropic foundations that help support them now control nearly one-third of all the productive property in the nation."

"I have read that statement and heard it repeated."

"How can you justify that kind of selfish use of private property?"

"I can't because I don't believe it," Wilson said, "although the amount of property controlled by the 2,000 or so colleges and universities must be substantial. Even if it were true, it would be human and not diabolical. Education should be every man's responsibility to himself and to his children and collectively through these to his neighbor and his neighbor's children. He should pay for it daily or at least annually. But it is human to forget to pay, and it is human of those placed in charge of education to amass wealth for their institutions for protection against the public's neglect. Just as it is human for men and women in this audience and perhaps even on the jury itself to condemn me for a crime in which they themselves participated—and honestly believe that I am guilty."

After the uproar subsided, Wilson added, "What your question means to me, of course, is that you and Senator Bartlett have the same economic reason for burning the universities as King Henry VIII and his fellow rulers had for confiscating church lands in the Middle Ages." Wilson smiled. "My former colleagues in economics would be smiling if they were here."

"I do not care what your former colleagues would be doing," Kelley said savagely, "nor what this question means to you. Nor does this excellent jury that you have slandered with your filthy accusations or the vast American audience care for this farcical justification for your criminal actions. A man on trial for his life should not be cynical."

"A prosecuting attorney should not be making speeches during cross examination," Wilson said mildly.

Kelley turned off his anger as quickly as he had turned it on. "I understand that you are a sociologist, Wilson."

"A physicist and then a sociologist."

"What is a sociologist?"

"He is concerned with the development and evolution of society."

"He wants to know why groups of people act the way they do?"

"That's part of what he wants to know."

"And what if he should find out, Wilson?"

"People could construct better societies. They could learn how to live together without conflict and frustration, getting out of society the satisfactions they need and putting back the fuel that society needs."

"You mean, don't you, that sociologists could construct societies they thought were better?"

Wilson said, "You turn to a doctor when you are sick because he knows more about sickness and health."

"And knowledge is power, isn't it, Wilson? If I know why a group of people does something it is only a small step farther to knowing how to make the people do it—or do something else."

"Well, yes," Wilson admitted, "but sociologists wouldn't—"

"Why wouldn't they? Wouldn't you construct a better society if you could, a society in which the universities would not burn?"

"I suppose—"

"Are the rest of us to trust our lives to the benevolence and wisdom of the sociologists? Or the psychologist? If a psychologist knows why a person acts the way he does—if he really knows instead of guessing a little better a little more often than the average person—the next thing he can do is make a person act that way, or some other way. Give a psychologist that power and you take away free will from the rest of us. People don't want that to happen. You don't want it, Wilson. I don't want it. Nobody wants to be a puppet; they want to be people; they want to make their own choices, their own mistakes. They don't want to live somebody else's idea of the good life."

"Nobody wants—" Wilson began.

"How do you know what nobody wants? You want to build a better society. The psychologist wants to build a better person. But who knows how to build a better sociologist, a better psychologist? Who knows how sensible you are? How sane you are? Who gave you the power? The people do not want you to know that much about them. Before they let you know that much they will burn you!" Kelley's voice had climbed steadily until it was almost a scream at the end.

Wilson looked at him in amazement. "What you are saying is that ignorance is preferable to knowledge. It may be bliss, but it is a dangerous bliss that threatens its neighbor as well as itself."

But very few could have heard Wilson. The courtroom was in an uproar. The judge's gavel was banging on his bench.

At last when relative quiet returned, Wilson said, "You

are talking about mere animal survival; I'm talking about the glory of being human."

Kelley's voice was deceptively mild. "That is your own coat you are wearing, isn't it?"

Wilson looked down, surprised. He fingered the lapel where he had once, in a moment of lucidity, concealed a razor blade. The blade was gone now. "Yes, I think so."

Kelley stepped forward and put his hand on the breast pocket. He pulled down hard. The pocket ripped—so artfully that Wilson thought it must have been carefully prepared for this moment. With the pocket came much of the jacket front. It revealed what had been concealed between the layers of cloth—a fan of thin, insulated wires. So much had happened since he put them there that he had forgotten, but Wilson remembered now the device he had gimmicked together in the desperation of his flight, a gadget adapted from his research which would pick up primitive theta brain rhythms in his immediate vicinity. The hearing aid he had attached to the antenna had long ago been discarded. He didn't need it now to pick up the theta rhythms of the audience, rapid, pounding. . . .

"Here is not merely a sociologist," Kelley was screaming. "Here is a scientist with a machine for reading minds—and perhaps, God forbid, for making others do his will!"

The audience roared in animal fury. They were out of their benches, fighting toward the railing. In spite of his training Wilson shrank back in his chair. But there was a man, a single man, who stood between him and the crowd—not Kelley, who had pulled back in front of the jury, but a man who had been sitting in the group behind Wilson's table. Senator Bartlett himself, in his worn, gray coat and his ragged blue shirt open at the collar, held back the crowd.

"Gentlemen," he implored in his unctuous voice. "Ladies! This man is on trial in a court of law. No matter how heinous his crime, he deserves a fair American trial. Not only the nation but the world is watching. He must be convicted legally, not lynched by a mob."

Slowly they fell under the mesmeric spell of his singsong phrases. The television cameras came up close to study Bartlett's face. Wilson, however, was not present for the end of the scene. Guards had closed around him, hustled him out the door with the frosted glass and then out the back way and into the waiting truck. In a moment it had pulled away and was speeding toward the highway, leaving the old courthouse behind.

"Well," Kelley said, "you gave us a little surprise there, didn't you? Almost pulled it off, too. Who got the antidote to you? The girl? I suppose. It doesn't matter, though. You're going to die in a very public and edifying way. Put him out, Doc."

And someone pressed an anesthetic gun to his arm and pulled the trigger. It was a drug for which he had received no antidote or for which the antidote he had received had worn off. The world faded away.

IX

Someone was shaking him by the shoulder. "Wake up, Mac," said a rough voice. But that was not the start of it. Even before the shaking and the voice that urged him out of his dark isolation, he had felt the bite of a needle into his arm, or his subconscious remembered it. "Shake out of it, fellow," the voice said impatiently. "We gotta go."

The sting of his arm had roused him out of a vivid dream of that world which he now accepted as a dream world. He had been standing in the imposing entrance of the City Hall. Its ceiling towered 40 or 50 feet above his head.

Around the edges of the central lobby had been the soldiers. Huddled within the circle formed by the soldiers were a hundred spectators, mostly villagers with a sprinkling of ragged city dwellers. A soldier stood on either side of Wilson. In front of him was the dark young man. He sat in a tall chair. Between them was a charcoal brazier. From the coals that glowed in it a thin, almost invisible column of smoke spiraled up to be lost in the dim heights of the ceiling. On the coals the large, blunt tip of a soldering iron with a wooden handle was beginning to turn red.

"John Wilson, are you a witch?" the young man asked in a stern voice. The audience drew a deep breath.

"I am what I am," Wilson said.

"Are you a witch?" the young man asked again.

"I am a man, no more, no less," Wilson replied.

"Are you a witch?" the young man asked the third time.

"If I were a witch," Wilson said, "you would not dare my wrath, Captain Leonard Kelley."

The audience moaned. The young man drew back in his chair, his index finger and his little finger making horns at Wilson with his right hand. His face was rigid and his eyes narrowed. "If you know my name, you know it by witchcraft," he said. "But I do not fear your power, nor will I condemn you without fair trial. Hold out your hand, John Wilson."

Wilson held out his right hand. Kelley picked up the soldering iron and moved it gently through the air. Smoke curled from the glowing tip. Kelley passed the iron in front of Wilson's face. Wilson could feel the radiant heat.

"If you can hold the iron and not be burned," Kelley said, "you are a witch and you will be placed in a fire prepared for you in the plaza outside until your power is overcome. If you do not accept the iron, you are a confessed witch and you will burn. John Wilson, do you confess?"

"I confess that I seek truth and serve the people," Wilson said, "and because of these things I will accept the iron."

Wilson held out his hand. Kelley hesitated and chewed on one side of his lower lip. "Take it, then!"

He placed the still-glowing iron in Wilson's hand. The audience groaned and surged forward only to be met with the upraised weapons of the soldiers. "Calm yourselves, friends," Wilson said clearly, although his hand smoked and waves of pain coursed up his arm toward his head.

Kelley sank back in his tall chair, staring at Wilson with dark eyes, his hand covering the lower part of his face.

"And what if I accept the iron and burn, Captain Kelley?" Wilson asked.

"Kill him!" Kelley said.

The spectators surged forward.

"You gotta wake up," said the voice again. "We got no time."

Wilson opened his eyes and looked at his right hand. It was pink and unmarred. He wiggled his fingers. They moved freely. He had only the memory of pain, but it still seemed quite real.

A man was bending over him, a man in prison denims of gray and dark blue. Beyond him the sliding bars that formed the door to his cell were pushed back. The door was open. Beyond the door was the wide corridor between the cell block and the stone outside wall, lit feebly now against the night by light bulbs high in the ceiling. The barred windows were dark.

"We're breaking out of here," the man said, moving back a little. "Strange things're going on—men have seen fire balls drifting outside and one guy said he saw one inside the walls. I don't know why but the guards're gone. Come on, Mac. Get up and let's go."

"That's all right," Wilson said. "I'd just as soon stay here."

"Mac, you don't know what you're saying. They're gonna hang you."

"How do you know?" Wilson asked, interested.

The man shrugged, his shaggy eyebrows moving high on his forehead. "We heard the radio reports on our earphones. No jury could do anything but find you guilty, the announcer said. That's the word, brother, believe me!"

"You'd better go on," Wilson said. "I'm going to wait for whatever comes."

The other caught his right wrist in a strong right hand. He pulled Wilson upright. "You don't know what you're saying, Mac. We ain't gonna leave nobody here."

Wilson pulled his wrist free. "Try to understand, fellow. I'm conscious, and I'm turning down your invitation. I'm grateful for your concern, but—"

The other's fist caught him on the jaw before he could finish. As consciousness fled Wilson could feel himself falling.

Wilson lifted his head as the men half-carried him down the broad steps. Subconsciously he counted them as his feet bumped down each one. "Forty-two," he said at the bottom and didn't know why he'd said it.

Fifty feet from the bottom of the steps was a tall guard house shaped something like a lighthouse. Wilson

couldn't see a guard in it, but he thought he saw something else in the shadows behind the glass panels at the
top—something with one staring eye and a small red eye
beneath—but he couldn't be sure.

Beside him and around him other men were moving.
He could feel them in the darkness and then he saw them
clearly as a ball of red lightning drifted around the corner of the tall penitentiary building and passed near them
before it swerved toward the guard house, clung to the
knob at the top for a few seconds, and dissipated.

The heat of the evening was oppressive and still, and
the clouds were low. "Just the night for a tornado," Wilson muttered.

The group of men in whose midst he was moved along
turned toward a truck parked nearby in the broad driveway that circled the guard house before heading back
toward the distant town. Suddenly men in uniform began
coming around both corners of the building. They came
endlessly. "Stop!" said a voice amplified into a giant's
roar. "Don't move! If you try to escape, you will be shot
down. Stop where you are!"

Wilson looked back up the steps. More men in uniform
were coming through the doors they just had left. One of
them carried a portable amplifier held to his mouth.

Down the long double driveway past the guard tower,
lights began to flicker like giant fireflies. The men with
Wilson didn't stop. They continued toward the tarpaulin-
covered truck, but others began to scatter. Some of them
ran to the left across the open lawn. Others sprinted out
to the right.

"For the last time, I warn you! Stop where you are!"
said the giant's voice.

Guns barked. Searchlights came on, holding men pinned
in their beams like butterflies against a black velvet
mounting board. Men crumpled in mid-stride. Others staggered on until they, too, were knocked to the ground.
Some were whirled around by the shock of the impact.
Others turned and held their hands in the air.

The group of men with Wilson was almost to the truck
now. Just before they reached it the tarpaulin in the back
parted. The men with Wilson stopped. The dark young
man named Kelley was in the back of the truck, and
more guards and more guns.

"Here he is," said the man who had been in Wilson's cell.

"And here is your reward," Kelley said.

A gun went off and another. The men near Wilson began to drop away. The man who had spoken looked to the right and left bewildered. "But you said—" he began, and then he, too, started folding himself up.

In a moment Wilson was standing alone. He felt his sore jaw. "Aren't you going to shoot me, too?" he asked.

"We're going to do better than that," Kelley said and motioned toward the driveways.

The fireflies had turned into torches, and the torches were at the head of twin crowds of men and women. Hoarse voices reached his ears. They were singing something. Men with portable cameras ran along beside the crowds.

Guards were on either side of him. They boosted Wilson into the truck and pulled the tarpaulin back against the cab. There, his back braced against the cab, was Senator Bartlett. He did not move as the truck started up and pulled slowly down the driveway. Wilson staggered and caught himself.

"Hello, Senator," Wilson said.

Bartlett's arms were folded across his chest. "You're a strange man, Wilson. We could have chosen better."

"Everybody agreed he was the one," Kelley said defensively.

"I'm not blaming anybody," Bartlett said. "But the way things turned out, we could have chosen better."

"I would gladly have had this cup pass from me," Wilson said.

"You are a blasphemer as well as a meddler," Bartlett said. "No wonder the people hate your kind."

The voice of the crowd was closer. The song was "The Battle Hymn of the Republic."

"They will hate anybody," Wilson said, "but you have done your job well. And profited thereby."

The truck stopped, backed in a curving path, and turned in another curve so that its back was toward the crowd. The crowd's torches created a ragged hemisphere of light. Beyond it the blackness struggled to return.

"I do not lead," Bartlett said, his gaze turned inward. "I am pushed. The people tell me what to say and what to do, and I say and I do what they tell me. They say that the eggheads must die if the people are to live, and the eggheads will die." It was as if God had spoken.

Bartlett stepped to the rear of the truck to face the crowd. A murmur ran through it as the singing died away. The murmur turned to cheers and shouts of "Senator! Senator!"

Bartlett held out his arms for silence. Standing between two guards Wilson could see the cameras focused on the Senator's flame-lit face and outstretched arms. It was a familiar pose. Wilson had seen it often on television and in publicity shots. It brought back the memory of the night the university had burned.

"People!" Bartlett said. He said it quietly but his voice carried well. Wilson decided that he had a pickup in his artfully aged coat. The crowd roared and slowly returned to silence. "My people!" The crowd roared again. "Disperse, I ask you now! Go to your homes! Leave this man to the law!"

"No! No!" the crowd shouted. "Burn him."

Beyond the crowd Wilson could see a tall pillar and a pile of crates and boards around it, still growing as men tossed more wood on the pile.

"I honor your feelings in this matter," Bartlett said. "The man did try to escape, to evade his proper punishment. But I ask you to forbear. A second time I ask you, leave him to the law!"

"Burn him! Burn him!"

"This man is guilty," Bartlett said. "We all know that. The verdict is a formality. But I ask you to hold your hand, restrain your honest wrath. Leave him to the law!"

"No! No! No!"

"Then if you must have it so, I give this man to you for justice. Let him die for what he has done! Let him burn for the torment he has given others! Let him perish along with all others of his kind! Let his fiery end be a warning to the rest! The people will not be ruled by any except themselves.

"This man is guilty of treason to the people. He has betrayed you. He has tried to steal your minds and twist your thoughts. Let him burn!"

Bartlett ended with his arms spread wide once more. His arms dropped to his sides, his head drooped like a wilting narcissus, and he stood aside. Wilson was pushed forward by the guards.

"I can walk," Wilson said, but they would not let him. He was shoved from behind, and he fell into the crowd. Head high the men and women carried him toward the post. Hands clutched at his clothing and tore pieces of it away and, he thought from the twinges of pain, pieces of himself as well.

In a moment they placed him upright against the pillar which was, he discovered, an old fence post. Someone pulled his arms behind the post, tied his hands together, and hammered something into the post. When he couldn't move his hands up or down he decided that the rope had been nailed to the post. "Hang on tight!" someone said in his ear. Wilson tried to see who it was, but the man was gone.

Then a man came forward with a torch.

"People!" Wilson shouted. They quieted slowly and the man with the torch hesitated.

"Go ahead," someone urged from the back. The man with the torch started forward again.

"I came back," Wilson shouted, "to die if I must, but I did not come back to die. I am ready to die because we all are guilty, but it will not help you to kill me. You will be killing part of yourselves—the part that thinks, the part that makes you human. Know what you do! When you abandon reason and commit yourselves to terror, you can be certain of only one thing. You will never know what tomorrow brings. You may be next. You—"

And then the torch plunged into the crates and boards at his feet. They began to smoke and to crackle. In a moment they had sprung into flame and Wilson took a deep breath of air before it, too, turned into flame.

He was trying to decide whether it would be better to hold his breath as long as possible or to breathe in the fire and shorten the end when he noticed the crowd stirring around him, looking behind rather than at him. Over their heads as they cringed aside came a blue ball of lightning. It came straight toward Wilson and settled on the post just above his head. Wilson could not see it then, but he could feel it, electric and almost cool, behind him. It must make him quite a sight, he thought, as he wondered how long it would be before the flames began to consume his legs.

Miraculously, however, the post began to move, slowly at first and then with greater speed, pulling him up and away. He felt the strain on his shoulders as if they were about to be dislocated, and he hugged the post tight with all his strength. The flames dropped behind, below. He could see the faces of the crowd looking up at him like curious saucers with shadowy eyes and noses and mouths painted on them.

"Shoot!" somebody shouted below. It sounded like Kelley. "Quick. Shoot him!" But the barking of the guns was seconds too late. He felt a bullet pluck at his tattered clothing, and then he was into the low-hanging clouds and into something else, and hands grabbed him, something cool and wet was sprayed onto his legs and feet, and he was drawn back onto a bench or cot.

Wilson looked around. He was in the belly of some kind of airplane. In front of him an open doorway in the floor was closing. From the way it hovered, Wilson thought it must be a helicopter, but it was remarkably silent. To his left was a man he had known as Pike. In front of him was Youngman. To his right was Pat Helman looking as desirable as ever.

"Surprised?" Pat Helman said.

"Pleasantly," Wilson said. "I wasn't expecting you."

"That's the best kind," Youngman said.

"That was quite a fireball," Wilson said.

"The ball lightning was just for show," Pike said. "A strong black wire did the real job, just like in the magic shows."

"What were all Bartlett's and Kelley's last-minute shenanigans about?" Wilson asked.

"They were losing in the courtroom and on the tube," Youngman drawled. "They had to wind it up fast and dramatically or find themselves on the losing side—and once those kind start to lose they go down fast, like Danton and Robespierre."

"You're joking," Wilson said.

"You underestimate your powers of persuasion," Pat Helman said. "You're quite a man, John Wilson."

Wilson looked at her. "I wonder how persuasive I could be." He turned to Youngman again. "Was it worth it? Did we do any good?"

"Our best estimate is that it will slow them down," Pike said. "Nothing will reverse the trend. That must wear itself out. But we may have eased it off a little. Maybe we can save a few more victims. At least the stage is set for the next act."

"Was the last act to your satisfaction?" Wilson asked. His voice had an edge to it.

"We're not stage managers," Youngman said. "We just hang around to pick up the pieces and try to keep the edges of the conflagration dampened so that it doesn't spread too fast. You've had the toughest part, but don't forget that Pat and I had our necks out there, too."

"Sorry," Wilson said. "What is the next act?"

"We have to start work in the little towns, the little out-of-the-way places," Pat Helman said. "The consensus is that we should establish ourselves there as witches, if you will, or witch-doctors with the power to help the people control the unseen and the unknowable, while others go in search of truth and find—"

"Don't tell me," Wilson said giddily. "I know all about it."

He was feeling very strange. He was just beginning to realize that the martyrdom he had accepted had indeed passed him by, and the relief made him feel weak and somehow ashamed of his relief and his weakness. He thought about how he must have looked to the crowd as he rose, with his halo of ball lightning, toward the clouds. The apotheosis of John Wilson, he thought.

And he recalled how close the flames had been and fainted. It was a habit that would be hard to break.

PART THREE

WITCH HUNT

I

The pilgrim stopped on the bridge that spanned the muddy river and leaned on his green staff. The original bridge had been constructed of reinforced concrete and resurfaced many times with asphalt, but the roadway had fallen into the river in places and the entire span had been recovered with rough beams of wood.

Beyond the end of the bridge the market town began. The pilgrim could not put a name to it. Some market towns in this part of the Empire had squares; others had broad main streets. This one had a broad main street.

Although there never was one shop that looked quite like another, the shops in one market town looked exactly like those in the next. A few stone and brick structures remained from before the time of starvation, but most of the shops had been built since the time of troubles. They had been put together with salvaged beams and boards mixed with new, uncured planks that disliked their neighbors. The timbered houses had upper stories that overhung the streets.

The pilgrim turned and looked back the way he had come. The highway crumbled its way out of sight in the distance. Out there somewhere it crossed under the four-lane turnpike he had followed much of the way from Denver. From here the pilgrim could see the high bridge of the turnpike which spanned the entire river in one clear arch but whose roadway was completely gone, leaving little but a lacy iron skeleton. The pilgrim had crossed it rather than work his way through the ruins and the underbrush.

He had come to the timbered bridge along the highway, past old buildings fallen in upon themselves, past ancient middens in which, if he dug, he would find much rust, much broken glass, and strange, indestructible objects of materials no longer found in nature.

The pilgrim's face was gaunt under the gray cowl. A scar from a recent wound crossed his right cheek. His eyes were watchful and observant.

It was time to forget the past for the moment, he thought, and concern himself with the future. He stepped off the bridge into the town and wondered what wisdom it would bring him.

The noise of the town reached him first, a muted roar that seemed to the pilgrim, after his long absence from civilization, like a voice from a single throat. It grew louder as he walked toward it and then began to differentiate into individual voices: peddlars crying their wares, shoppers bargaining with shopkeepers, quarrelers shouting at each other, musicians competing for gratuities, beggars soliciting alms, blacksmiths, tinsmiths, coppersmiths hammering out their wares. . . .

The smell of the town came to him, a strong odor of sweat, spices, and decay. A gout of fluid splashed at the pilgrim's feet. He looked up and saw a basin disappearing into an overhead window and a shutter closing, and he shouted, "Hey, look where you're throwing!"

"Look where you're walking!" he was told in the shrill tones of a woman.

The pilgrim drew up his dampened robe and shrugged. It was the middle of the afternoon, and the fluid that flowed in the gutter likely was washwater, not nightsoil.

And then he was in the town proper, with its shop windows proclaiming what the town lived upon: at the ironmonger's there were scythes and sickles, shears and baling hooks, spades and hoes; at the cooper's there were bee hives and churns, milking stools and pails, hay rakes and kegs; at the wheelwright's there were carts and wheelbarrows; at the saddler's there were saddles and harness and horsecollars; at the chemist's there were horse embrocations; and at the cobbler's, heavy shoes and boots for trudging across furrows.

The pilgrim did not look long at the shop windows. Life was swirling around him, as multicolored as oil on

water. In the broad main street were villagers in their
dirt-stained overalls, shopkeepers in aprons, townsmen and
women in fancy bright garments exaggerated in line and
ornament, a minstrel or two singing about the old days
when men could fly, a band of players posturing and
mouthing meaningless words resurrected from some ancient classic, mercenaries swaggering with their swords
swinging from their hips, an almost naked Luddite stalking
a poor frightened blacksmith's apprentice the Luddite had
mistaken for a Neo-Scientist, a soldier or two in the Emperor's livery. . . .

While he was watching the dazzling display, the pilgrim
did not notice the arrival of a horse cart until it was
abreast of him. He drew back into a doorway, but the
cart passed and stopped a little farther down the street
where a fight had begun between a mercenary and a
soldier over the favors of some painted townswoman. Before the soldiers could pile out of the cart and reach the
two, the mercenary had plunged his sword through the
soldier and faced the newcomers with his dripping blade
cutting bloody circles in the air.

The soldiers stood well away from the sword and leveled
their pellet guns at the mercenary. Slowly the mercenary's
rage ebbed, and at last he tossed his sword to the sergeant
in command of the squad and let the soldiers take him.

The pilgrim did not see where the soldiers took the
mercenary or what they did with him. He did not have to
see; he knew the Emperor's justice and the Emperor's
mercy. His attention, however, was distracted by a loud
roar from the direction of the river, back the way he had
come. An open truck loaded with watermelons was sweep-
ing downriver making a spray of water on each side like
a thousand legs and a wake behind like that left on a still
pond by a giant waterbug. When the truck reached the
bridge it nosed up over the bank and climbed to street
level and came down the street, blowing dust even more
furiously than it had blown water.

The people in the street sauntered away toward the
shops and turned their backs to the gale, scarcely pausing
in their conversations. Then the truck pulled up in front
of an open market for garden produce, decreased the volume of its thunder, eased down on its inflated pads, and
shut off its witchpower entirely.

In the comparative silence that followed, the pilgrim

turned to the shopkeeper behind him and asked, "What do you call this town?"

"Lawrence."

"And this street?"

"People here always have called it Massachusetts, but no one knows why."

"The Allegheny Republic has a place called Massachusetts," the pilgrim said.

"Is that so?" the tradesman asked politely. "May I sell you a linament, an embrocation?"

The pilgrim smiled, but the right side of his mouth drew up more than his left and his expression looked more like a sneer. "I have no horse save shank's mare," he said, "and the last six months have toughened her wonderfully."

From nearby came sounds of scuffling followed by a protest in what sounded like a girl's voice or a young boy's and the rough questions of a man.

"You are a girl!" the man said.

"A woman!" the other responded.

The pilgrim turned toward the street. Not far from him was a figure cowled and robed in gray monk's cloth like himself, but slighter in build and stature. Beside that pilgrim, holding one arm, shaking it for emphasis, was a mercenary with an unruly head of blond hair and a yellow beard.

"You know the difference between a girl and a woman?" the mercenary said. He pulled the other pilgrim close to whisper in an ear.

"None of your business," the pilgrim said.

"But it is the business of every man with every woman," the mercenary said, and laughed.

"You'll never make it around," the pilgrim said.

"I'll die trying, and I'll die happy."

"Try this woman," the pilgrim said, "and you'll never have a chance to try another."

"Pilgrims are supposed to seek experience."

"We seek truth. Let go my arm."

"Pilgrims are not supposed to be girls."

"There's no law," said the pilgrim, twisting out of his grasp and moving down the street.

"But there is," said the mercenary, striding to catch up. "Natural law. What has not been should not be."

"Go away," said the girl. The pilgrim was sure now

that it was a girl. He had caught a glimpse of her face as she passed. Not only was it a girl, it was a girl he knew, too well. He had known it even earlier, as he heard her voice. He pulled himself back farther in the doorway.

"Not unless you go with me," the mercenary said, catching her arm again.

"Molest not the pilgrim," said a farmer, gripping and re-gripping a sickle he had been testing at a shop.

"Let the pilgrim go in peace," said another farmer, stepping up beside the first.

"This is no honest pilgrim," the mercenary said. "Look!" He flung back the girl's hood. "It is a girl masquerading as a pilgrim, profaning the robes she wears."

"I'm an honest pilgrim," the girl said, "seeking the truth as well as any man, and when I find it I will know it as well as any man because I have been to the witch schools and studied well. . . ."

The first farmer scratched his neck. "I never knew a girl to be a pilgrim."

"There are many," the girl said, "although not so many in these parts as elsewhere, and not so many as there are men, who can better be spared—"

"I never knew a woman pilgrim either," said the second farmer.

"You see?" the mercenary said cheerily. "You might as well come along with me. You have no future in this pilgrim line." His voice softened. "Come. Even though you look like a boy and are stubborn as a mule, you appeal to me. I'll treat you kindly while we're together and leave you no worse, I do believe, than you are now."

He began to pull her toward a nearby tavern, but she reached up her free hand, snakelike, and sank her fingers into his face. Just as quickly, he swung his right hand and cuffed her to the ground. As she lay on the decaying rubbery surface, he brought his right hand to his face, wiped the blood, and looked at it on his fingers.

"I like spirit in a woman but not spite," he said. "But I'll soon beat that out of you."

He reached again for her arm but found his hand blocked by a green staff. The pilgrim was standing half between them.

"Do not interfere, pilgrim," the mercenary said. "I

would not willingly injure someone of your calling, but I will not stay my hand from one who gets in my way."

"The girl is a pilgrim," the pilgrim said. "She said so, and I tell you so. And if she were not I would not willingly see you take by force any unwilling woman."

"You are a fool, pilgrim," said the mercenary and reached for his sword.

Before the hilt had parted from the scabbard, the pilgrim's staff had swung around to rap him sharply on the wrist.

"Fight!" came an outcry from up and down the street. "The pilgrim and the mercenary fight!"

The mercenary released the sword handle and nursed his wrist with his left hand. "It's broken, I think, damn you!" he said. But as he said it he was lunging toward the pilgrim with a knife in his left hand.

The pilgrim stopped him with a jab of the staff to a spot where his ribs joined, and then the other end of the staff whipped, whistling, through the air to smack solidly against the mercenary's skull.

The mercenary dropped like a puppet whose strings had been released. He lay in the street, breathing raggedly, senseless.

"Good for you, pilgrim," someone said.

"Soldiers are coming. Better leave," said another.

The pilgrim did not move. He looked down at the girl. She was sitting up, rubbing her jaw. With her cowl down about her shoulders and her brown hair cropped short, she looked as much like a boy as a girl but there was something unmistakably feminine about the contours of her face and the delicacy of her features.

The pilgrim reached his hand down to help her to her feet, but she knocked the hand away and scrambled up without aid.

"You got away," the pilgrim said.

"Obviously. And so did you," the girl said.

"But we can't seem to stay apart."

"Nobody asked for your help," she said.

"Where have I heard this all before?" the pilgrim said. "I've gotten into this frightening habit, and I find myself involved before I know it."

"The soldiers," someone shouted from the crowd. "They're here."

There were six of them, in uniform, fully armed, work-

ing their way through the crowd. The pilgrim turned back
to the girl, but she was gone and so was the senseless
mercenary, who, it seemed, was senseless no longer.

The further progress of the soldiers was blocked by
farmers standing shoulder to shoulder.

"Make way," the sergeant said.

"You'll not take the pilgrim," one of the farmers said.
"You'll not take one who was only protecting a girl from
a mercenary and spilled no blood."

"Make way here in the name of the Emperor!"

"A pilgrim has immunity," said another farmer. "He
cannot be tried in the Emperor's courts."

"The captain will be the judge of that," the sergeant
said. "We'll take him in, and if he's innocent he'll be released with no harm."

"You'll not take the pilgrim," the first farmer said.

Above the heads of the soldiers, floating down the
street, came a flaming orange ball of witch fire. One of
the farmers pointed at it. "The witches have come to
claim their own."

The soldiers fidgeted, but the sergeant said, "The witch
fire never has been known to harm anyone. We'll take the
pilgrim whether you let us or no. Men, take aim!"

"Wait," the pilgrim said. "Let them through. I'll go
with the soldiers. I have no fear of the captain or the
Emperor's court."

"You don't know this captain or this court," a farmer
muttered. "It'll not be fair or pleasant."

"I wish to go with them," the pilgrim said.

The farmers parted. The soldiers moved between them,
grabbed the pilgrim's arms, and hustled him toward the
waiting cart.

"Do not mistreat the pilgrim," a farmer called after
them, "or the witches will take care of you."

A shudder ran through the two soldiers holding the
pilgrim. They feared the witches but not enough to let the
pilgrim loose. They feared the sergeant more, and the
sergeant feared the captain. Who did the captain fear?

The pilgrim looked off down the street. The city hall
was evidently the old, white stone and red brick building
several streets away. Beyond it, built on a hill, he caught
the distant glint of a witch's chapel rising above what
must be a witch-doctor's villa.

The cart lurched off down the street, the witch fire

sitting on the right front post. No one dared brush it aside.

II

The pilgrim walked down the right side of the divided highway which in some places, for some forgotten historical reasons, was called a turnpike and in others an interstate. He breathed in the good morning air, winy at this altitude. He enjoyed the warmth of the bright sun, alone in the blue sky. He swung the green staff he had cut in a stream bed a few miles back where he had enjoyed his breakfast of sausage and bread a farmer had given him, washed down with mountain water.

The highway was in good condition here. Although the weeds on each side were chest high, the black rubbery substance with which the ancients covered many of their roads was still relatively intact, marred only by an occasional patch of grass which had grown through a crack or lodged in a dirt-filled crevice.

For the hundredth time since he had started along this great highway that bisected the Central Empire, he wondered how the ancients had built it and all the lesser roads of which relics remained. Perhaps it had not been built by men at all but by witches and witchcraft. The witch-doctors said not. They said that once men used machines that did all work for them.

And they had died for it, the pilgrim reflected.

The witch-doctor with whom he had studied would not have agreed. "There is no evil in machines," he said once. "There were only evil people who used machines or weak people who were used by them. If you can learn this much, you will know more than all but a few of the people you see around you, for their ancient fears are strong."

"That's not hard to learn."

"You are a strange man," the witch-doctor said. "Some people might call you cynical or amoral. I think you are brilliant and have not yet found anything to believe in. And when you do—the universe had better watch out.

Others are different. What they cannot understand, what they can never hope to do themselves, is magic—they must consider it magic if they are to live with it at all."

"I think it is time men built machines again. Or they will die, as they have lived, futilely."

"You do not know people," the witch-doctor said. "You must go live among them when you begin your pilgrimage, to get to know them as well as to seek truth, to learn why a few among them can do as you say but the many cannot, and you must decide how to separate the few from the many."

The pilgrim stretched his arms out wide as he walked, feeling strangely joyous this bright morning, as if this morning great revelations would come to him, he would find the truth or part of it. He walked now where strange machines once had hurtled, if the old tales were to be believed, with their cargoes of men and animals and priceless goods. The tales had to be true, he thought, for how else would one explain these roads used now only by an occasional foot traveler, a cart, or a farmer's truck floating to market.

It was ironic, he thought, that the farmers of the Empire rode swiftly and the soldiers of the Empire, even the Emperor Bartlett himself, traveled no faster than a horse could go. But the Emperor had seized trucks and used them briefly and within months they had lost all power and were worthless. Some said that the spell wore off. The Emperor did not believe it. But the brave men who tried to explore the workings of the trucks died horrible, wasting deaths.

Ahead of him the pilgrim saw the beginnings of a wooded area. The highway had fallen into a river, and trees had grown up around it and through it until the roadway had virtually disappeared. The pilgrim debated trying to find a way around the woods, thought better of it, and made his way between the trees.

The trees were largely cottonwoods and thorny locusts with a few oaks scattered among them. When the wind blew, the cottonwood leaves rustled like sheets of paper being rubbed together. The air which had been clean and clear now was thick with the odor of growing things and the fishy smell of the river.

For a little way into the woods there was a path, but it petered out among the trees and the underbrush, and the pilgrim had to make his way alone. After half an hour he was beginning to think he would have to turn about and try to find his way back to the path when he heard voices ahead and broke from between the trees into a clearing.

In the middle of the clearing was a small house built of roughly sawn boards. It had a thatched roof and a smoking chimney at the near side. Beyond the house was a small garden plot; a pig was rooting in it. In front of the house was a group of three men wrestling with a girl whose long brown hair swung wildly as she struggled silently with the men. Another man stood at one side and watched. It was he who said quietly, "Let her go. We have a visitor."

The other three swung to face the pilgrim, but one of them continued to grasp the girl's wrists. They were ragged men wearing what had once been the Emperor's uniform. Deserters, the pilgrim thought. Perhaps outlaws in other ways by this time.

"Forgive me for breaking in upon you like this," the pilgrim said. "Please go on with whatever you were doing and I'll go back the way I came."

"We can't let you do that," said the quiet one. "You might bring other people before we're finished here. I think we'll have to tie you up like the old man."

"I don't think I'd like that," the pilgrim said. He noticed that two of the three men who had been struggling with the girl had recent scratches on their faces. "I think we'd all be happier if we went our separate ways."

"You fool!" said the girl. "Let them tie you up!" Her face was earnest and intense and quite pretty, the pilgrim thought, but a little too willful for his taste.

"If he will not persuade, we must use stronger arguments," the quiet one said. "Sam, you approach him from the right. Jones, you take the left. I'll be in the middle. If he tries to run he won't get far in the underbrush. Watch the quarterstaff! A man with a quarterstaff may know how to use it."

"It's the worst of bad luck to harm a pilgrim," the pilgrim said, watching their eyes as he talked. The quiet one's eyes were steady and blue and focused unwaveringly on the pilgrim's staff. He had drawn a short sword from his belt and had it in his hand. The one called Jones had shifty little eyes and a ferret mouth at which ferret teeth gnawed continually. He, too, had a sword, but it was raised to strike rather than to thrust like their leader's. The one called Sam looked dumb and sleepy. He had a club.

"Well," said the quiet one, "we aren't trying to harm you, you know, only detain you for a little. And we don't know for sure you're a pilgrim, even if you are wearing a cowl. And, anyway, the way our luck has been running it couldn't get much worse. So, if I were you, I'd throw down that staff before you get hurt—accidentally."

"Speaking of luck, there's some blue witch fire on the chimney now," the pilgrim said.

None of them moved their heads, but the pilgrim thought he detected a flicker of uncertainty and struck. The staff whacked Jones on the wrist, making him drop his sword, and the other end whipped around to thump the leader on the head. But before he could swing the other end against Sam, the club hit the side of his head and he went down. The last thing he saw, or thought he saw, was a ball of witch fire actually sitting on the chimney.

When the pilgrim awoke, his head throbbed and his shoulders ached. He knew why his head throbbed. His shoulders ached from being pulled back by the hands tied behind him. He opened his eyes, but he couldn't see anything. The air was close and full of the odors of cooking and living, and he decided he was inside the little house. He tried to wriggle upright, but his feet were bound, too.

"So you're awake now," the girl said. Her voice seemed weary and truculent at the same time.

But it was close and the pilgrim wriggled toward it until his body came up against something softer than a wall. "Yes," he said quietly. "Where are they?"

"They've finished with me for the moment," she said, "so now they're getting ready to torture my father to make him tell where he has hidden the gold."

"Why doesn't he tell them?"

"He doesn't have any gold. Nobody has around here anymore, but myths survive a thousand fatal blows. The Emperor's soldiers won't believe us, and now these! All my father has is me and a bad heart. Why didn't you stay out of this?"

"I couldn't very well keep from stumbling into this clearing."

"Most people would. They wouldn't come blundering in. If you had peeked cautiously, you could have gone on without harm. We'd all have been much better off."

"I thought I might get a little gratitude for trying to protect you."

"Rot! You were trying to protect yourself."

"True. But why would you have been better off?"

"Those men were deserters, but they weren't beyond decency. All they wanted when they stopped was some food and a kiss or two."

"You were struggling!"

"That's my decision and my responsibility. You had no business making us pay for your actions."

"Suppose they hadn't stopped at a kiss or two?"

"Would I have been any worse off? You are a meddling pilgrim! If you'd only let them tie you up, even then it might have been all right, but you had to be a hero. You sprained the wrist of the mean one and made him meaner. And you stunned the leader who had kept them from going wild, who wanted them to move along. He hasn't said a word since.

"They've raped me three times, and after they kill my father they're going to kill you and take me with them until they tire of me. And it's all your fault."

"I didn't bring them to this clearing."

"You brought yourself. That's disaster enough."

They lay on the rough floor, back to back. The pilgrim felt the splinters against his cheek, smelled the wood fire burning in the next room, and listened to the sound of the girl's angry breathing.

"Well," he said, "we'd better do something about it."

"What?" she snapped.

"Do you have any feeling left in your fingers? If you do, see what you can make of these knots on my wrist."

"They feel just like a mess of twisted ropes," she said after a short pause.

"Feel them some more," he urged. "Try to become familiar with them, the way they twist and turn under each other. Memorize them with your fingers. Visualize them in your mind."

"I'm doing it," she said.

"These men were soldiers, and the army teaches its

soldiers that there's only one right way to tie a knot. See if you can find a rope end."

"I've got it."

"Does it go under another rope?"

"Yes."

"Then pull on it, firmly and steadily, and pray."

The pilgrim felt the tug of the rope, felt it loosening, and then his hands were free. "Good," he whispered. He sat up and undid the ropes around his ankles and then turned to the girl.

Voices came from the next room. "The iron's ready. Get the old man."

The pilgrim felt the rope give under his tugging. And then the girl struggled, and the rope tightened again. He slapped her on the shoulder. "Quiet!"

Another voice said, "I can't wake him up."

The ropes around the girl's wrists fell away, and she was trying to get up and hop toward the door. The pilgrim pulled at her bound legs and caught her as she fell, one hand clasped across her mouth. She struggled in his arms.

The first voice spoke again. "He's not asleep. He's dead. Cold."

The girl stopped struggling.

"Now get those ropes off your legs," the pilgrim said, releasing her.

He moved to the door, catching himself as his right leg, asleep, almost crumpled under him. He stood by the door, smelling the wood smoke, flexing his fingers and wiggling his toes.

"Maybe the girl knows something."

"If she does, she won't tell you. She's the most stubborn girl I ever saw."

"Well, let's get rid of the pilgrim, take the girl, and get out of here."

The door opened and firelight spilled into the room, exposing the girl where she sat struggling with the ropes around her legs. She looked up, blinking, peering about. The one called Jones stepped into the room, peering about. "The damned pilgrim's gone," he called back over his shoulder, and the pilgrim hit him and then caught the handle of his sword as he fell to the floor.

The deserter known as Sam already was running forward, and the pilgrim did not underestimate his speed this time. He lunged with the sword's point and caught him in mid-stride. The dull, sleepy eyes looked down at the blade stuck in his chest, and the body crumpled at the knees and fell forward.

The pilgrim wrenched the sword free as it fell and continued his lunge in two swift steps across the floor. He cut down the deserter by the fireplace who was holding a hot poker in his hand. That was the one who had clung to the girl.

The pilgrim looked to the left. The quiet-voiced leader was standing in the doorway, his sword in one hand, the doorframe in the other. He had a bandage around his head. "Not this time, pilgrim," he said. "I'm not myself." And he disappeared into the night.

The pilgrim turned to follow. As he turned he felt a blow to his right arm. It stung, and he turned, tossing the sword to his left hand, to find behind him the deserter called Jones, a knife upraised to strike again.

The pilgrim cut him across the middle and dropped the sword to clutch his right upper arm. It had begun to burn, and he could feel the blood pour out of it hot and sticky. He squeezed it tight.

"Well," the girl said, standing in the doorway and looking at the bodies in the room, "you are a bloody pilgrim. Is violence your only calling?"

The pilgrim looked at her incredulously, and then a wry smile began to curl the corners of his lips. Only the right side rose a little higher than the left and his smile looked like a sneer.

He wavered a little on his feet, looked around, and sat down heavily on a crude chair. The girl ran to the bunk to the right of the fireplace. She picked up the hand of her dead father, held it, looked into his face, and turned back to the pilgrim.

"The sly one got you, didn't he," she said. She came to him and pried his fingers away from the wound and spread apart the hole in the rough shirt he wore under his robe. "It's an ugly wound." She rummaged in a cabinet in the corner and came back with a strip of white cloth. "Here," she said, binding it tightly around the arm.

The pilgrim felt a little dizzy.

"Now get up," the girl said briskly, "and let's get you to a witch-doctor. He can give you some powders and have that sewn up so it will heal within a week. Come on, now. Don't fall back."

The pilgrim stood, swaying. "How far is it?"

"Only five miles," she said, and caught him before he sank back into the chair.

III

The trip through the dark forest was a nightmare of pain and fatigue and dimming consciousness, but at the end of it was light and warmth and comfort.

The witch-doctor's villa looked small from a distance. You could see it from a distance because it was lighted at night, as was the silolike chapel behind it. Up close, however, the villa seemed much larger, and inside it seemed interminable.

It had an odor all its own, a blend of antiseptics, something that smelled like—the pilgrim could find no word for it but "energy"—and a trace of oil.

"Come in, Susannah," the witch-doctor said after the door had announced them. "Come in, son, and let's have a look at that arm."

Wordlessly, the pilgrim held it out, winced as the witch-doctor detached the girl's bandage, bit his lower lip as the witch-doctor probed at it. But even in his pain the pilgrim was studying the man.

The witch-doctor was dark where the pilgrim's mentor had been fair and short where his mentor had been tall, but in spite of the difference they seemed as much alike as two men might be. There was about them both an aura of inner certainty, as if they had arrived at an answer which explained everything and they need question themselves no longer. Or perhaps, as the farmers thought, they were the favorites of the world's unseen powers and, being all powerful, could afford to be generous and kind.

"Come into the clinic," the witch-doctor said. "You, too, Susannah. You're a graduate and may see such things. And you, young man, are a pilgrim."

"Yes."

"Where did you study?"

"Near Denver."

"And who was your witch-doctor?"

"He was tall and fair and wise. Witch-doctors have no names."

"Nor do pilgrims, and I will not ask yours."

The witch-doctor eased the pilgrim down flat on a table fashioned from some slick, dull-finished metal the pilgrim had seen only in the witch's villa near Denver. The witch-doctor eased his arm onto a shelf and brought forward from behind the table an object on wheels which fitted entirely over the arm.

"It was a pity about your father," the witch-doctor said as his busy hands attached vinelike objects to various parts of the pilgrim's body.

"How did you know about my father?"

"One never asks a witch-doctor how he knows." But he smiled. "We have our ways. You'd better take one of those blue pills on the second shelf there."

"Why?" the girl asked.

"In my day, we used to call them 'morning after' pills. Take one. Those men didn't hurt you, did they?"

"Them?" Her head tossed scornfully. "It would take a hundred like them."

"Good. They can't hurt you, not the real Susannah. Now, young man, I can't say this won't hurt at all, but it won't hurt much." He pressed a button. Something buzzed. "You're in good shape. But it will take a little time for you to recuperate. How long have you been on your pilgrimage?"

"Three months."

"And what have you learned?"

"I have not yet found the truth, but I have learned that people are pretty much the same all over, some good, some bad, some kind, some cruel. They all want something, and if they want it too much, they turn bad, and if they don't want anything very much they are the prey of those who do."

"You have learned a good deal. How would you change the world to make it better?"

"You must have more of everything, so people's wants can be more easily satisfied, or you have to rule more firmly so that evil is deterred."

"And suppose there was a place where there was more of everything, but it was a place that took a great deal of getting used to—a place where not everybody could live?"

The pilgrim hesitated.

"That's easy," Susannah said. "You let those live there who can adjust to it—"

"And rule everybody else more firmly," the pilgrim finished.

"A remarkable combination," the witch-doctor said. "There—your arm is ready." He pulled back the object on wheels.

The pilgrim lifted his arm. The pain was gone, there was a new bandage on the wound, and the bleeding had stopped. But his head swam as he sat up.

"I'll take you home," the witch-doctor said. And he ushered them through the seemingly interminable villa which always gave the pilgrim the impression that it had subterranean powers beneath it that throbbed just below the level of audibility. And finally they came to a brightly lighted room in which sat a miniature version of the farmer's truck except that it was slimmer.

The witch-doctor and Susannah helped the pilgrim into a front seat and then got in on either side of him. In front of them a wall opened up, and with a quick roar and a whoosh of air the witch's broom took off for a quick ride through the dark paths of the forest.

As they left the clearing in which the witch-doctor's villa was located, the pilgrim turned to take one last look. The villa stretched across between the trees, and the tall, pointed chapel was behind.

"What do you see?" asked the witch-doctor.

"An enigma," the pilgrim said and was silent.

At the cabin the witch-doctor and Susannah helped the pilgrim get out and into a bunk. He was asleep almost before his head touched the corn-shuck mattress. Minutes later—or perhaps it was hours—he was awakened by someone entering the house. He felt for his staff and found nothing. He turned on his side and groaned as his arm stabbed him with pain. Then he opened his eyes and saw Susannah. She was standing in front of the fire, leaning on a shovel and gazing into the flames."

"Where have you been?"

"Outside."

"What have you been doing?"

"Burying," she said.

And he nodded and turned on his back and went to sleep again.

A week later his arm had healed. He could swing it freely without pain, and there was only a pink scar where the knife wound had gaped. The pilgrim walked out into the clearing and stretched in the sunshine.

"You're well," said the girl, behind him.

The pilgrim nodded. "Time to continue my pilgrimage."

"That's what pilgrims must do," she said.

The pilgrim wondered if there was a note of wistfulness in her voice. If there was he would ignore it. She had been pleasant enough during their seven days together. She had cooked their meals, cleaned the cabin, tended to his wound, hoed the garden. And she had hummed as she did these things. It was all too cozy.

The pilgrim did not trust anyone, particularly women, who enjoyed labor. They must have motives, he thought, and he suspected motives, even his own.

He went to a nearby oak tree and cut himself another green staff about six feet long. He held it experimentally, his left hand about a quarter of the way from the end, the right hand about the middle, and maneuvered against a cottonwood sapling, ending with a solid and potentially crippling blow to the sapling's middle.

He walked back toward Susannah, inspecting the staff for cracks and splinters, finding none.

"Here's your robe," she said, holding it out. "I washed it for you. And here's some cheese and fresh bread I baked this morning. You can eat it for your lunch when you come to a quiet stream. If you go that way—" she motioned with her head toward the far end of the clearing, "—you'll reach the interstate directly."

"That's good," the pilgrim said. "I'm grateful to you for nursing me and for taking care of me." He slipped into the robe and once more felt like a pilgrim.

"That was nothing," she said. "You rescued me from the deserters. You may even have saved my life."

"That wasn't what you said when we were tied up."

"You did that after we were tied up," she said. "I don't approve of killing. None of our family ever approved of killing. I had a brother who became a pilgrim."

"You never heard from him?"

She shook her head. "Either he found truth or death found him. I like to think he found truth."

"If he had, wouldn't he have come back to tell you?"

"No pilgrim ever returns."

The pilgrim was anxious to be away, but somehow he felt that he hadn't acted sufficiently grateful or sufficiently concerned about her welfare. "What will you do now?"

She sighed. "I thought you'd never ask." She reached behind the door to bring out a gray robe with a cowl. "I've decided to be a pilgrim, too. I'm going with you."

"That's impossible."

"Nothing is impossible in this wonderful world."

"Oh, I've heard of women pilgrims, but never a man and a woman together."

"I could cook and wash for us both, and you could find food, and we would have more time for seeking truth. We would find it that much sooner."

He shook his head. "Pilgrims travel alone. And even if they didn't, I travel alone. And even if I didn't, I wouldn't want to be responsible for you."

"I need nobody's help," she said. "I'm responsible for myself."

"Stay here," the pilgrim said. "Or go to the witch-doctor and ask him what you should do."

"He said I could be a pilgrim. He said I should go with you."

"Go ahead then. Be a pilgrim! But be one somewhere else!" The pilgrim turned and walked briskly toward the far end of the clearing and strode into the forest.

He had not walked far when he came to the highway again. He thought of it as a friend he had not seen for a long time. He began to walk along it, heading east, breathing the winy air and enjoying the morning sun. But after a few minutes he had an uneasy feeling in his shoulder blades and looked back. Following him was another gray-robed figure.

He waited for Susannah to approach. "I thought I told you not to follow me," he said.

"No, you didn't. What you said was, 'Be a pilgrim somewhere else.' And that's where I am—somewhere else."

"Then I'm telling you now. Don't follow me."

"A pilgrim must go where his conscience leads him. My conscience tells me to follow this road, for now."

The pilgrim turned and walked briskly away. He kept up a good pace for as long as he could and then stopped to pant. He glanced back. The girl was only a few paces behind and she wasn't even breathing hard.

The pilgrim turned and walked on at a more normal pace. A little past noon, by the sun, he came to a stream and stopped to drink from his cupped hand, took the bread and cheese out of an inside pocket of his robe, unwrapped it, and began to eat. He ignored the girl who, ten feet away, was going through the same ritual. When he finished he brushed away the crumbs, drank again, stood up, and walked on. The girl took up her place again, ten paces behind him.

All afternoon the pilgrim had the feeling that the girl's gaze was burning itself into his shoulder blades. He had the self-conscious urge to shift his back, and only the strongest of will power kept it still. That was painful.

In the early afternoon they came to a village—no more than a dozen buildings clustered on the near side of the road. Beyond were level fields, turned now in the spring for the planting of corn and vegetables. In some of the fields the winter wheat was up, a shimmering green across the land. In a distant field a truck was spreading witch powder to enrich the soil or to kill weeds or pests, and in another a truck was pulling a cultivator.

There was a scattering of people in the village, dressed in working clothes still stained from the fields or the household chores. They were talking to each other or bartering idly for goods. No coins changed hands. In all such villages, the pilgrim had never seen any coins. He had asked why this was so and he had been told—for everyone answers the questions of a pilgrim for in what they say he may find truth—that what they did not have the Emperor could not take away. Besides, bartering was their pleasure.

Now they called to the girl walking behind him.

"Susannah, you're a pilgrim now."

"I heard about your father, Susannah. Such a pity."

"Stop and stay a spell, Susannah. We'd be proud to have you."

And to the pilgrim, they said, "Welcome, pilgrim. Stop with us. Share our evening meal."

Then the pilgrim turned the corner of a building and saw beside it a horse-drawn cart. The cart was filled with cabbages and beets and apples, carrots and sacks of grain and potatoes, and a pig. Beside the cart stood a sweating sergeant and behind him seven soldiers, each with his arms filled with produce.

"But we don't want your food," the sergeant was protesting to a villager who kept trying to thrust upon him a clucking chicken. "We want gold, coins, whatever you have. We don't have room for all this food. We would have to walk, and my soldiers must be ready to fight at all times."

"Sir," said the villager, his white hair shining in the sunlight, "we have no gold. The last of the Emperor's soldiers through here took all our remaining ornaments, although many of them were only brass, and now we have only food. But you are welcome to that and more. Please take this chicken with our best wishes. Take her to the Emperor. She will make a good meal for him with dumplings."

The sweating sergeant caught sight of the pilgrim. "Pilgrim, maybe you can make him understand. Tell this poor savage that we can't take the food."

"What brings you here, sergeant?" asked the pilgrim.

"Chasing four deserters," the sergeant said. "But we were told to collect taxes on our way, as usual. Have you seen them? The deserters?"

"Yes. I killed three of them."

"You killed three of them?" The chicken dropped out of the sergeant's hands. It ran off to join its flock, gabbling about its reprieve.

"There was a big one, a rough one, a sly one, and a quiet one. I killed the first three. The quiet one got away."

"Why did you kill them?"

"They attacked me."

"You're a mighty lethal pilgrim. You'll have to come with us. Men, get that stuff out of the cart. We're going to take this one in."

"It's unlawful to interfere with a pilgrim," the pilgrim said.

"Not when he's committed murder, and it's murder until those men were officially tried and convicted."

"Which you and your squad would do when you found them."

"But we didn't find them, did we?" said the sergeant. "Besides, they'll never believe us at headquarters if we come back and tell them some pilgrim killed Sam and Jones and Upshaw. Not unless we produce the pilgrim who said so."

"I liked Sam," said one of the soldiers.

A small group of villagers had gathered around them. Susannah pushed her way through them. "You should take me, too. I'm a pilgrim."

"Did you kill anybody?" the sergeant asked wearily.

"No, but they—they attacked me, and that's when the pilgrim—I'm a witness—"

"It doesn't matter," the sergeant said. "We haven't got room for more than one prisoner."

"But I'm with him," Susannah said.

The sergeant looked at the pilgrim. He shook his head.

Susannah clung to the sergeant's arm. "You don't understand. He saved my life and now he's responsible for me."

"That's a vicious philosophy," the pilgrim said.

The sergeant flung her to the ground. "Get in," he said to his men. They caught the pilgrim by his arms and helped him into the cart and found places for them all on benches along each side. The sergeant got into the seat in front and urged the horse into motion, leaving behind them a heap of produce and a squealing pig. The cart turned right and headed east on the highway.

After they had traveled a mile or so down the road, the pilgrim looked back. The village had disappeared but a small, gray figure was trudging after them. In another half-hour the figure had disappeared.

IV

By mid-morning of the following day the hard wooden benches had become like flint beneath the pilgrim, and for that reason alone he wished he had made an effort to escape during the night, even though he had been shackled to a snoring soldier on either side as they slept.

What kept the soldiers in condition to fight? he wondered.

They had been traveling on the high plains. Now they began to pass through a series of low hills. On one of them the pilgrim glimpsed a lone horseman silhouetted against the sky. When he looked again, there were a dozen there. He pointed them out to the sergeant.

"Luddites," the sergeant said. "They won't attack. They fear the Emperor's wrath, and they know his guns. They'll wait for some lone traveler or some poorly armed group. Naked cowards!"

They passed on, the horse wearily pulling the heavy cart as if it knew its fate and was resigned to it. Over hills and between hills they went until suddenly, as they were between two high stone hills, a metal fence rose up out of the ground in front of them to a height of ten feet and then twenty feet.

The horse braced his feet to stop, but the weight of the cart kept pushing him forward until the sergeant remembered to help with the brake.

"Back!" he shouted. "Everybody out and get turned around." But by the time the cart was swung around another metal barrier had closed the way they had entered.

"Everybody get their guns," the sergeant shouted. "At the ready!"

"If you reach for your guns," said a clear voice from above, "I will have to blow you out of there."

Everyone looked up. Seated in a chair supported over the roadway by a metal boom was a man in a white jacket or robe. It reminded the pilgrim of the white jacket worn by the witch-doctors, but it was fuller and longer.

In front of the man was a board on which his hands rested. He wore on his face some glass objects which magnified his eyes until he looked like an owl. On his head was a white cap which completely covered his hair.

"On the hills beside you, you will notice, are the mouths of instruments of destruction," the man said. "You will believe me if I tell you that I have but to press a button and those instruments of destruction will belch fire and steel into this small valley until there is nothing left of it. If, by chance, one of you might make it to the barrier, you will find that something frightening and fatal will happen. Like this!"

He tossed his hand toward the barrier the cart faced. A length of something metallic flew through the air and struck the fence. It flared brightly, melted, and fell in separate pieces to the ground.

"You are frightened by this new force, right?" said the man in the chair above them.

"A Neo-Scientist!" the sergeant said.

"You are correct. And one day my colleagues and I will be greater than the scientists of old, who called this energy in the barriers 'electra-city.' Now, throw your weapons as far from you as you can."

The pellet guns flew in all directions.

"Now the knives."

A few knives followed.

"One by one you will climb the ladder which will descend to you." The Neo-Scientist's hand pressed against the board in front of him and a ladder uncoiled over the edge of the hill. The sergeant went up first. At the top he hesitated as if he were deciding whether to take his chances in the valley behind him, took a deep breath, and went on. His soldiers followed him.

The Neo-Scientist turned to the pilgrim. "It went very well, didn't it? Everything worked perfectly. It was the first time, you know, so I couldn't be sure. But it did go well. Didn't it?"

"Well, yes," said the pilgrim.

"Come up the ladder, then. You are different from the others. They are workers. That is their function. You are an educated man, a seeker after truth. That is your function. You could be a Neo-Scientist, if you wished. You are my guest. If you decide to join me and explore the unknown, we will rejoice. If you wish to go on and find the truth in your way, we will be sad for ourselves but happy for you."

The Neo-Scientist pressed his board again, and the boom swung back behind the hilltop as the pilgrim climbed the ladder. When he reached the top, the Neo-Scientist was there to grasp his hand and help him up.

The pilgrim stood up, stopped, and stared. Below him was a small city built on the edge of a bright lake. Smoke came curling from chimneys, people rode carts through the streets, and the carts had no horses pulling them, a big structure built of wood was drilling something into the earth, crews of men were building roads. It was a lovely picture of civilization and industry, and the pilgrim blinked. He had thought that nothing like this existed on earth any more.

"This," the Neo-Scientist said, "is New Pittsburgh."

"Pittsburgh," the pilgrim said, "is a place in the Allegheny Republic ruled by the Hereditary Governor of New York."

"Today it is a large village surrounded by ruins," the Neo-Scientist said. "This is the New Pittsburgh, which one day will be bigger and more prosperous than the old Pittsburgh."

And the pilgrim believed him until he looked down and saw the sergeant and the soldiers being fitted by white-coated men with metal collars fastened one to another by metal chains.

"My own invention," said the Neo-Scientist. "At any moment, those collars can be charged with a variable amount of electra-city. A small amount and the collars only tingle: a warning. A larger amount and the collars shock: punishment. At the top limit they can burn and kill: example. We have very obedient workers."

"I believe you," the pilgrim said. "Do you have many workers?"

"Ten for every Neo-Scientist. In New Pittsburgh everyone has a job, a function. The Neo-Scientist's job is to think, to explore, to invent, to make life easier and progress possible. The worker's job is to provide the Neo-Scientist with the time to do these things. Woman's job is to produce more Neo-Scientists and workers. If everybody does his job, everybody is happy."

"Can slavery work?"

"It is a matter of function," the Neo-Scientist said. "In nature everything has a function. The grass grows, the rabbit eats the grass, and the wolf eats the rabbit. The ants in the anthill, each has his job, and when all do their jobs the anthill thrives, and when the anthill thrives all the ants in it are happy. It is when man ignores function that he becomes unhappy.

"Besides, I am working on a brain operation which will allow me to implant an electrode in the happiness center. When a workman does his job he will be allowed to stimulate himself for an appropriate length of time."

"And what will happen when the Emperor finds out about New Pittsburgh?"

"Do you think his soldiers could stand up against my

instruments of destruction—the electra-city, the big guns? Watch." He bent over the chair in which he had been sitting and turned a knob. "Look toward the other hill." He pushed a button. The black object exploded and produced a gout of red flame and black smoke. Thunder enveloped them. Something whistled into the distance. Something exploded above the distant hills.

"And do you think he could stand up to my workers, armed with superior weapons and urged on by the stimulation of their collars?"

"Perhaps not," the pilgrim said. "But he would try. And I know he would give much to gain control of your weapons and your method of worker control."

"Ah, but what would he do with them?" the Neo-Scientist asked. "He would only do more of what he does now: control more land, rule more people. What will that prove?"

"But where does all of your work lead?"

"To man's destiny: the discovery of all truth."

"Is that the witch-doctor's truth?"

"They have one truth. We have many, as many as there once were people on this earth. Do you know how many people once lived on this world of ours?"

The pilgrim shook his head.

"Four billion people lived on this earth because of the machine. The entire world was like New Pittsburgh, filled with machines that did all the labor. Then men had time to think and solve the mysteries of the universe. And they solved many of them. We find bits and pieces of their solutions that survived the time of flames when the Lowbrows rebelled and ran the eggheads, and the time of starvation and time of troubles that followed when almost four billion men and women and children died of starvation and privation and violence. The old scientists thought they could just let people run loose, doing what they wished. See what happened. The machine was broken, and we have this backward world which can support no more than 100 million people or so.

"But we can profit by the example of the past. We search the world for the science of the past and go on from what they learned to discover the truth of everything."

The Neo-Scientist clearly was serious. "That is a noble ambition."

"It is a noble race."

The Neo-Scientist motioned the pilgrim to get into a small, open car with four seats in it. It rested on rails near the top of the hill. When they were both seated, the car began to move smoothly toward New Pittsburgh below.

The sergeant glanced at them as they departed. The pilgrim thought his eyes were haunted.

"How do you determine who are workers and who are Neo-Scientists?" the pilgrim asked.

"Everyone gets the same education until they are eleven. At eleven they take an aptitude examination. The ones that pass go on to a Neo-Scientific education, as high as they can go. A few drop out along the way and become technicians. The rest are fitted with collars and put to work."

"That must be a moment of great terror."

"Not at all. What they dread more than labor is further education. Using their arms and backs comes more naturally to them than using their heads. Function!"

By the time the car on rails had reached the outskirts of New Pittsburgh, the town did not look so attractive. The smoke from the chimneys hung in the air, making breathing difficult, settling on the houses, dirtying roofs and clothing, peeling paint off the walls. The horseless carts were emitting choking fumes, as well. The roads were rutted and full of holes. Even the bright lake had a gray scum along its shore. It extended several hundred yards into the water.

And the people who were working did not look up as they passed.

As they rolled through the town, the pilgrim's impression of despair grew. At the end of the rails was a building faced with massive columns and twined with ivy. Rising from that base was a tall, white, windowless tower.

"Come," said the Neo-Scientist, descending from the vehicle.

They went through broad doors and into a large, marbled lobby. Clerks rushed up to the Neo-Scientist, waving messages at him. Neo-Scientists came toward him in their smocks, asking questions. He waved them all away.

"We have a guest," he said, "this earnest pilgrim who, like us, is seeking truth. Speak with him, answer his questions, share your confidences and your thoughts with him as you would with me, and perhaps he will join us."

Then the Neo-Scientist led the pilgrim to the far wall in which there were many doors. The Neo-Scientist pressed a button. One of the doors opened. They entered a little room. When the door closed, the room began to move upward. The pilgrim had a feeling of greater weight. He counted twenty doors before the room stopped, the door in front of them opened, and they emerged into a spacious hall.

The Neo-Scientist led him to one end of the hall, opened a door, and showed the pilgrim into a comfortably fitted sitting room with an adjoining bedroom and bath which disposed automatically of waste fluids and other materials. There were books in the sitting room dating back to before the time of burning, and there was a mechanism which he could use to call for food or companionship.

"My rooms are at the other end of the hall," the Neo-Scientist said.

It was a more astonishing building than the Emperor's palace in Denver and more luxuriously appointed.

"Why do you build so high where there is so much land?" the pilgrim asked.

"You ask good questions. That is a most promising sign in a young man. There are many reasons for building a tall building like this: first, it concentrates control and information processes in a small space; second, it impresses the people with the permanence of their leaders; third, it pleases the populace like the pyramids of ancient Egypt or the skyscrapers of ancient New York; fourth, it has a virile symbolism; fifth, it inspires the occupants to strive harder for understanding; and sixth, it places the leaders far from the scene of possible violence. There, I have been frank with you as I always hope to be, and as I hope you will be frank with me."

"I hope to be."

"Now I have much work to do. If you need anything, just call into that instrument. And remember: funcfion!" And he closed the door.

Clearly, this was one possible answer to the riddle proposed by Susannah's witch-doctor. This was a place where there was more of everything. It took some getting used to. He supposed that a lot of people could not live there; they would not like the tall building, and they would hate or not be able to tolerate the machines. So the Neo-Scientists adjusted to it, and everyone else was ruled firmly.

But somehow the pilgrim did not think the witch-doctor was referring to New Pittsburgh.

And he went over and put his hand on the door, and the door would not open.

It was locked. The pilgrim felt a moment of panic until he remembered the mechanism on which he could call for food or companionship. He called for food, and when he had eaten he called for companionship. When the young Neo-Scientist came he strolled the streets of New Pittsburgh with him, talking about the town and how it was to live there and about science and the new life that was building.

The pilgrim spent seven days in New Pittsburgh, talking, living a carefree, comfortable, intellectual life, and in spite of the obvious degradation of the many he could not help being fascinated by the equally obvious liberation of the thinking man to do that which makes man most human.

Then he would watch the workers in their collars, and the mercenaries who acted as foremen over them, twisting the knobs on their control sticks, and standing guard at the outskirts of town.

And the pilgrim could not help noticing that whenever he was alone in his room the door was locked and whenever he was outside the room someone was with him. After a little he began to wonder if he too did not wear a collar like the workers, only he had fashioned it and put it on himself.

On the evening of the seventh day, after dusk, as he was walking with one of the young Neo-Scientists, he talked with him about the mysteries of the earth and about the mysteries of the sea, about the mysteries of the air and the mysteries of the stars. He began to grow very excited about the human adventure.

In the distance came a chorus of loud yells, and the pilgrim saw a group of flickering lights. He heard a thunder of hooves getting closer, and he wondered what new miracle New Pittsburgh was producing.

V

The hooves became separate horses, the flickering lights became individual torches, and the yells parceled themselves out among the individual throats of near-naked Luddites who were storming down the main street of New Pittsburgh. They tossed their torches into houses, and the houses magically turned into flame, and the flames painted the bodies of the Luddites. The Luddites leaned far over from their horses to club down pedestrians in the street. They took particular delight in smiting a mercenary or a Neo-Scientist. And they swept up a few women to ride behind them on their horses.

Two of them saved their torches for the buildings adjoining the Neo-Scientist tower, and then it seemed as if the entire city had turned to fire and men and women were running frantically back and forth in front of the flames, not knowing what to do.

Everything happened so quickly that the pilgrim did not have time to evaluate his actions or reactions, and before he could do so a horse galloped so close by that its sweat sprayed on him, a strong arm closed around him and suddenly he was sitting on the back of a wildly galloping horse.

He thought of struggling, but he looked back and saw that New Pittsburgh was doomed. Everywhere it was burning, and even the tower of Neo-Science was in danger of being engulfed. Black figures were fleeing.

The last vision of the city the pilgrim took with him was of the sergeant and his squad of soldiers. The sergeant had found a saw, and he was sawing away at the chain that linked him to the next man.

The horses ran long after they had swept into the outer darkness and the ruddy light had faded into night behind them. Finally they stopped and the pilgrim was allowed to slide, leg and bottom weary, to the ground. The women were told to build a fire. They looked until they found some twigs and many cow chips. Then they were given grain and preserved meat out of leather pouches, and the Luddites produced a pot in which to cook them.

The pilgrim had been sitting back in the shadows, but one Luddite noticed him and urged him to join the other women. He urged him with a brisk blow to the back of the head. The pilgrim's cowl fell back.

"I'm not a woman," the pilgrim said.

"By damn, you're not," the Luddite exclaimed. "But you looked like a woman in that robe!" And he reached for a knife in his belt.

The pilgrim hit him just below his ribcage, and the Luddite grunted and doubled up. The other Luddites laughed until they rolled on the ground by the fire. "George and his woman!" they shouted. "George's woman has a kick like a mule."

The Luddite began to straighten up. He was still trying to get his knife out of his belt. The pilgrim hit him again in the same spot. The Luddite sat down heavily, and his fellow Luddites broke into new screams of laughter.

Finally the laughter began to subside. The stricken Luddite slowly began to get to his feet, holding his stomach and backing away. "Perhaps we can reach an agreement," he said. "I do not kill you, and you do not hit me."

"That's fair," the pilgrim said.

One of the other Luddites called out, "George, don't you know the difference between a woman and a pilgrim."

"A pilgrim? Is that what this is? I've heard of them but I never saw one before."

"One of them was in camp just a few days ago."

"I was out hunting with a bunch of the boys."

Looking around at the little group—there seemed to be no more than twenty-five Luddites, none injured—the pilgrim was astonished that so few had done so much damage.

After their simple meal of porridge enriched with bits of meat, they sat around the campfire talking in loud voices about the raid on New Pittsburgh, the destruction they had wrought, and the mercenaries and Neo-Scientists they had killed. There was no remorse.

When they had completed their boastful recounting of the evening's action, one of them stood up and began to chant a song of ancient bravery, of blows struck and victories won, of Luddites fallen in battle taking their enemies with them, of machines broken and of one vast machine that was stilled forever before it made slaves of all mankind.

"Machines must die!" he chanted. "Science must die! All who fashion and create must die! Man must live! Nature must live! And the right way to live will live!"

Later, as the talking died away, the pilgrim turned to the Luddite beside him. The Luddite smelled of smoke and grease and sweat, but the pilgrim was beginning to get accustomed to it. He supposed he was a bit gamy, himself. "Is that why you burned New Pittsburgh?"

"Was that the name of the place?" the Luddite said. It was George, his captor, who now had become his friend. "Well, it was for kicks, mostly," he said. "That's the way most of us look at it. A few, they really got this thing about the machine. They really go nuts about it. Not that we all don't feel kind of that way. Every moral person does."

"I suppose so," the pilgrim said.

"You've got to be for it or against it, our spiritualist says, and we Luddites are against it. We take sacred vows to destroy any machine we find and anybody who builds machines. You aren't a Neo-Scientist, are you? You were in that town."

"I had been captured, just as you captured me. How do you feel about the witch-doctors?"

"They're okay, I guess."

"Don't they use machines?"

"Naw," the Luddite said. "They got powers just like our spiritualists. You know—they can make the wind blow, heal the sick, turn the land sweet for growing things, bring the game, that sort of thing. It's all in knowing the right way of doing things."

"I see," the pilgrim said.

"Anyway, we don't see many witch-doctors."

Wrapped in blankets, lying on the sweet prairie grass that prickled a little through the blanket, smelling the fresh prairie air and the last smoke from the campfire, seeing the stars wheel past, they fell asleep.

In the next few days, the pilgrim became a part of Luddite life on the move. Given a spare horse, he soon became accustomed to riding it bareback, his robe floating out behind him like gray wings.

Where it was forested, they hunted the deer, waiting by streams until the spooky deer came stepping lightly to the trickling water for a drink. They fished for trout and bass and pike and, best-of-all for eating cooked over the campfire, catfish. And they chased a giant herd of wild cattle, felling them with arrows and lances as they rode along beside the running, plunging beasts. Afterwards, tired and dusty, they enjoyed a feast of steak and roast and liver and tongue cooked over giant fires and eaten until satiation, and they slept and woke to eat again and again.

It was a good, clean, manly life. The pilgrim felt himself growing lean and strong. His face became bronzed like those of his captors; soon the only thing that distinguished him from them was the robe he wore and would not discard. This was the way a man was meant to live, he thought.

In the evenings, after the meals were completed and the women were eating, the Luddites would talk by the fire about their exploits or sometimes about life and God and the afterlife. Sometimes the minstrel would sing of old glories or glories yet to come, and the blood would dance within each Luddite until he was compelled to get up and stomp around the dying fire as the minstrel chanted, making guttural sounds and whoops of other noise.

And the minstrel had made another song, a new song, about the burning of New Pittsburgh, and everyone sat quietly and listened.

Sometimes the pilgrim would show them tricks that he had learned—the boxing with the fists, the shrewd blows with the sides of the hands or the fingertips or the feet, the strange magic of the quarterstaff.

And then there would be long, quiet nights under the stars, wrapped in a blanket, for thinking or sleeping.

Perhaps this was the life the witch-doctor had meant in his riddle. It was a most pleasant life. There was plenty of what everybody wanted. But anybody could learn to enjoy it; except that there could not be too many or there would not be enough game or fish for everybody.

The lot of the captured Neo-Scientist women was not so ideal. But they were a subdued group good for little more than doing what the Luddites told them to do, gathering wood for fire, cooking meals, going with the Luddite who selected them to his blanket for the night. They did not complain much, however, although they got dirtier and greasier and more bedraggled each day.

There was little spirit in them, the pilgrim thought.

And finally, when the hunt was over, the riders came one evening to an encampment where wicker huts were built beside a stream. The riders came thundering down from the hill and into the camp, shouting and screaming. Out of the wicker huts came the women and children and old men and a few young men as well. They surrounded the newcomers with outbursts of joy and questions about the hunt.

"Later," George said. "Later at the campfire we will tell it all, the whole glorious tale. The minstrel has made a new song about our great feats of strength and guile and courage. It is a song that will live among the Luddites as long as there are minstrels with a voice to sing."

The pilgrim looked around for the other pilgrim and thought he saw a gray robe in the distance. While he was looking he thought he saw another familiar face, but he could not remember where he had seen it before.

So it was that the story was told at the campfire, after the feast on the meat the group had brought back from their hunting, and the singing and dancing went on long after the sun had set. But not for the pilgrim. In the crowd that spilled from the huts he had watched where the other pilgrim went, and now he sought the pilgrim out.

He pushed back a hood and said, "Susannah!"

"It's me," she said, wearily wiping one greasy hand across her forehead.

"What are you doing here?"

"Taking meat to the men."

"I mean in this camp."

"Seeking truth, and it is not here."

"You look thinner. Have you been sick?"

"Only of these savages. You'd look thinner, too, if the old women and the old men and the young men, too, beat you out of bed in the morning and sent you off to the fields to plant corn and potatoes with a crooked stick, shoo the birds away from the growing plants, pull weeds by hand, cook meals, wash clothes on a rock, and then be hauled off to his filthy blanket by one of these greasy pigs. But you seem to be doing well for yourself."

"I must admit I have found it a good life," the pilgrim said.

"It's a great life for the men. For the women it's drudging from dawn to the middle of the night."

One of the Luddite men danced by. "You want that woman? You can have her. No good for work, no good for sleeping with. Wear yourself out beating her and still she fights like a wild animal. You take her. She wears a robe like yours."

"There," the pilgrim said. "Now you are mine, and I will set you free."

"A great lot of good that will do me," Susannah said. "If I try to get out of here, someone else will grab me, and if I don't I'll have to work like the others or the Luddites will be turning on you."

"I suppose they couldn't have a double standard. Well, come with me. We'll find a spot to roll out a blanket and at least you can get a good night's sleep."

"I'd like to take a bath," she said.

"Don't they let you bathe?"

"When would I find time?"

"We'll both bathe. I haven't found time either. Where is a good spot?"

"Below the camp the stream has been dammed by beavers. There's a pool. We wash the clothes there."

In a few moments they were splashing in the pool together in the dark, rubbing themselves with sand and ducking their heads under to get the dirt and lice out of their hair.

When Susannah got out of the pond, the pilgrim was shocked to see by the distant firelight how thin she was and the bruises on her back and legs. He wrapped her in her robe and put on his own robe and found a level spot to spread his blanket. They lay down together on it, and he put his arm around her for warmth.

"You have had it tough," he said.

For the first time since he had met her she was silent. She put her head against his chest. Her body quivered. After a few moments the pilgrim realized that she was crying. He had had many experiences in this world, but he had seldom been alone with a crying woman and never with a woman who sobbed silently. He didn't know what to do. He patted her on the shoulder and said, "There, there." And when that seemed too paternal, he smoothed her short-cropped hair, noticing for the first time that she had cut it off. "It must have been terrible!" he said.

She cried harder, but eventually she quieted. The shoulder of his robe was soaked with her tears, but he let her remain where she was. Presently her growing warmth and her proximity began to work upon the pilgrim a familiar magic.

"Oh, hell," she said. "You're like all those other savages."

The pilgrim protested. "I haven't done anything."

"It's obvious what you're thinking. When you asked me to share your blanket, I thought you wanted me to get a good night's sleep."

"I did. Believe me. But you're so warm. I can't control my reactions, but I can control my actions. You have nothing to fear from me. An unwilling woman is not my idea of—"

"Oh, shut up!" she said, and she kissed him, and one thing led to another.

In the morning as the sun dazzled his eyes, the pilgrim awoke to find himself alone in the blanket. His clothing was gone, even his robe, and he had only the blanket to cover his nakedness. He felt around in the grass and found a wide, cloth belt. He strapped it around his middle and, wrapping himself in the blanket, went to the stream.

He found Susannah taking a blue pill out of a bag hung around her neck and popping it into her mouth. When she noticed him, she said, "I took a handful at the witchdoctor's while I was about it. I guess you think that's a terrible thing for a girl to do."

"Well, I guess not," the pilgrim said. "I mean, it's thinking ahead or— Anyway, it's none of my business." He stooped to drink.

Susannah said, "I'd advise you to drink above the camp. The Luddites throw all their garbage and other wastes into the stream."

She was beating his clothing between two stones. Her own clothes, still wet, were on her. "Do you want them to dry first, or wear them dry?"

"I'll wear them," he said. "I thought you hated this kind of drudgery."

"It's not drudgery when you're doing it for somebody you like. Besides, if I wasn't washing your clothes somebody would be beating me to work at something for them."

Turning his back, he slipped into his wet clothing and robe.

"It's a little late for modesty, isn't it?" she asked.

The pilgrim did not answer. He walked off in dignity, shivering, toward the camp. When he had drunk at the stream above the camp and picked up a couple of stray bones with meat on them to gnaw upon, he returned to the spot where he had left Susannah. But on the way he met an old woman who was whipping Susannah's legs with a bundle of switches and pointing off toward the fields.

"Stop that!" said the pilgrim. "This is my woman."

"Shameless man!" said the old woman. "Letting woman idle. Idle woman is evil woman. So say the wise men."

"Don't interfere," Susannah said.

He trotted along beside her. "What do you mean, don't interfere?"

"You must work within the system." Susannah scampered to keep ahead of the switches. "You can't fight it. Find out how it works, and then you can make it work for you. "I'm going! I'm going!"

The pilgrim searched out the Luddite named George. "Say, George," he said, "I want the pilgrim woman."

"Fine," George said. "You take her tonight."

"You don't understand. I want her every night—and every day, too."

"That's not the way it works around here," George said patiently. "Every woman is any man's woman. No favorites. No jealousy. No quarrels. Share and share alike. You have her one night; I can have her another night. Good system."

"But," the pilgrim said, "I—want her—for myself!"

"Well, you can't have her and that's that!"

A group of young Luddite men had gathered around the discussion, drawn by the straining voices. "What's the matter here, George?" asked the one who looked familiar to the pilgrim.

"This character wants a woman all his own," George said.

"How many do I have to fight," the pilgrim said resignedly.

"Are you some kind of spy?" George said. "We take

you in, we treat you nice, and now you want to change
the way we do things. Just like that! The old ways aren't
good enough for you. Are you a Neo-Scientist after all?"

"All I want is the girl," the pilgrim said, looking around.
But he wasn't quick enough. The club hit him on the back
of the head before he quite got the word 'girl' out of his
mouth. But he saw the man who hit him, and at that
moment he recognized who it was. It was the quiet deserter from Susannah's clearing.

He woke up with a frightful headache and someone
tugging at his hands behind his back. They were tied together, but as he realized that fact his hands fell apart,
and he sat up.

A hand came down over his mouth. He raised his
hands. The hand on his mouth was a small, shapely hand.

"It's me, Susannah," a voice whispered in his ear.
"We've got to try to escape. Tonight. They're going to
kill you. Slowly. With ceremony. That's their way. Come
on."

They slipped through a slit in the back of the hut and
crawled until they thought they were out of earshot and
then got up and began to run. They ran for a long time,
stumbling occasionally in the night, and threw themselves
down to rest and got up to run some more.

During the second rest Susannah said, "We'd better
split up. I think we'd have a better chance of getting
away."

"No!" the pilgrim said. "We both make it or neither
of us makes it."

"That's an idiot's choice," Susannah said scornfully.
"I'm not thinking of you. I'm thinking of me."

The pilgrim could not think of an answer.

They separated for the next to the last time.

VI

As the cart jostled through the rutted streets of Lawrence with the ball of orange witch fire perched on the right front post and the soldiers eyeing it furtively, the pilgrim thought over the events of the past six months since he had begun his pilgrimage from a village not far from Denver.

He had seen the way people lived. He had seen many kinds of people and many kinds of societies. He had known the life of a wanderer, and along his way he had met other unhappy, dispossessed persons. All the others, in their way, were happy or, at least, had something to recommend the way they lived.

The Neo-Scientists enslaved others but dreamed about the stars and the mysteries of life. The Luddites had a free, wild, wonderful existence free of most ordinary cares, but their life was only for men and it was always the same, one day to another. Maybe that was the way life was meant to be, the pilgrim thought.

The Empire was a joke. It did not seem like a joke when one was part of the court or near the Imperial seat where the Emperor's word was absolute. But beyond a radius of twenty-five to fifty miles people lived pretty much as they chose.

Then there were the villagers, most of them farmers. There probably were more of them than of any other kind. They raised their crops and their livestock, they went to the schools provided by the witch-doctors, occasionally a bright youngster would go off on a pilgrimage and never come back, and they were under the protection of the powerful but uncommitted witch-doctors.

The witch-doctors were the key to the situation, as the pilgrim analyzed it. They held power but they did not use it. They did not interfere. They helped when they were asked. They taught. They gave advice. They provided what was good for the body, good for the soil, good for the livestock, good for the mind. Maybe. But they did not interfere. They let the Emperor collect his taxes—if he could. They let people kill each other if they wanted to, love each other if that was the way their tastes inclined.

The pilgrim had never known them to lie, personally or through their teaching devices which gave answers and asked questions through some strange magic, just like a person. Occasionally both said things that were enigmatic or incomprehensible. Sometimes, later, some of these statements might make sense when he had learned something else.

The question: where did the witch-doctors get their powers? Did they, in reality, have some magic formula which brought natural forces under their command, some intercessionary power with the spirit world, if there was a spirit world.

Or, the pilgrim thought, were the witch-doctors like the Neo-Scientists? Were their powers completely natural, though beyond the scope of ordinary man, rather than supernatural? Did they manufacture and control machines?

If this was so, and the pilgrim was beginning to think that it was so, why were witch-doctors not set upon and destroyed by the Luddites and every other right-thinking person who remembered the time of starvation and the time of troubles. Both caused by the machine and the century during which it ruled the world. Why were they not killed like the occasional, aberrant Neo-Scientists who arose and had their brief day and were destroyed.

One reason: they did not glory in their machines like the Neo-Scientists; they built no monuments. Another reason: they did not explain; they called it magic.

Magic is acceptable; science is detestable.

The pilgrim felt an excitement growing in him: this was a truth that the witch-doctors sent out pilgrims to find. Magic is acceptable; science is detestable.

There was one catch: what did the witch-doctors gain by it? The pilgrim's excitement faded. There must be a profit; there must be a motive. Were the witch-doctors satisfied merely to do good so that others might live better lives? Did they get their return from the gratitude and admiration of the people, from their sacred positions, from the power to teach and preach? The pilgrim shook his head. Such saintliness was beyond belief. None of those motives were enough, not for him and not for any man, much less the thousands scattered in their villas across this empire and perhaps, who knows, across other lands as well, even to the mysterious Russias and the Chinas across the oceans that no one had heard from since the time of troubles.

And then the pilgrim's elation arose again. Perhaps the answer to the question of motivation was a second truth, or a complementary part of the first truth, and when one had learned this, one had learned the truth that one became a pilgrim to find.

Because there was, in the tradition of the pilgrim itself, some kind of return. This was, the witch-doctors said, the only way to become a witch-doctor. If you became a pilgrim and learned the truth, you became a witch-doctor.

Therefore—a pilgrim is a witch-doctor's way of making another witch-doctor, just as an egg is a chicken's way of making another chicken. But equally as true, a chicken is an egg's way of making another egg, and isn't therefore a witch-doctor. . . .

That was the wrong track. The question: what do witch-doctors do? They serve, said the witch-doctors. But that led back only to the village where the process began again. Do witch-doctors do anything else? Yes. They must. But if so, what—and where?

The pilgrim would have liked to pursue this line of reasoning farther, because he thought it was getting him somewhere, but the cart jerked to a halt.

"Out, pilgrim!" said the sergeant.

The pilgrim remembered another sergeant and wondered where he was now with his squad. He looked around. The city hall was an old brick and stone building. It must have been old at the time of starvation, the pilgrim thought, but it had survived the time of troubles better than newer structures, and its brick tower still ascended high above its stone front steps.

"Up! Go on up!" the sergeant said, yanking his arm. "The captain's waiting for you."

The pilgrim shrugged and walked up the worn steps and through two curious wrought-iron doors and up another short flight to a large room with tall windows on either side. All the windows but one had been broken many years ago and had been boarded up, but one miraculous window still admitted light. In front of its fading glory sat an officer behind an old desk, his sword laid across it still in its scabbard, scribbling away with a quill pen at a piece of paper.

The pilgrim looked around as they waited for the captain to complete his writing chore, and he noticed for the first time that the ball of witch fire had followed them into the building. It perched on a railing not far from the captain's desk, and the captain noticed it as soon as he looked up.

He would rather not have noticed it, the pilgrim thought. He would rather have stared overbearingly at the prisoner, but he saw the witch fire first and said, "Get that out of here!"

"How would I do that, captain?" the sergeant asked.

The captain was thin and red-haired and choleric. "Then get yourself out of here."

"This pilgrim is pretty good with a quarterstaff," the sergeant said. "Beat up a mercenary pretty good with it."

"Well, he doesn't have a quarterstaff now, does he?" the captain asked.

"What I meant, captain, was he might be good with other things, his fists, maybe."

"I can take care of anything he has in the way of exotic skills," the captain said. "Get out."

As soon as the sergeant had departed, the captain said, "The quality of non-commissioned officers you get these days is appalling. You'll have to pay a fine for brawling in the streets, you know. That will be two gold pieces."

"Which you will pocket," the pilgrim said. "Forget all that, captain. I'm on a special mission for the Emperor."

"And who might you be," the captain drawled, "to be doing a special mission for the Emperor?"

"My name is Leonard Kelley."

"Head of the Emperor's secret police," the captain completed for him. "And what is the nature of your mission, pilgrim?"

"That's my business, and the Emperor Bartlett's."

"I suppose you have identification."

"Of course. In my belt." He fumbled beneath his clothing for the belt, undid the buttons on it, and drew out nothing. He fumbled around in the empty pocket, thinking that he had not looked into it for several months, remembering the morning he found the belt beside his blanket. "I've lost it. Someone's stolen it."

"You've lost it," the captain said, resignation in his voice. "Pay the two gold pieces."

"I can give you corroborative information about the Court—"

"I've never been to Court, pilgrim. It would be amusing to see you trying to impress me, but I don't have the time. Pay the two gold pieces."

"Why would I try to make you believe a lie that could so easily be disproved?"

"People tell me the damnedest things, pilgrim. I've given up trying to guess why they do it. Pay the two gold pieces."

"Pilgrims have no money."

"I was afraid so. Why does that absurd sergeant keep bringing you beggars in here? Sergeant!"

The sergeant trotted into the room followed by four of his squad.

"Give this pretentious pilgrim a caning—five should be enough—no, make it ten. And then throw him out."

For a moment the pilgrim thought of making a fight of it, but he thought again and decided against it. He shrugged his shoulders and went with the sergeant fo a dingy cellar. It once had been something more than a cellar. It had had carved wood panels on the walls, but most of the panels had been wrenched away. Now there were cuffs fastened to the wall.

Two of the soldiers slipped his hands into the cuffs and fastened them. The sergeant removed his robe and tore his shirt down his back. He stepped back and chose a sturdy cane from a basket of them. He made it whistle through the air in preparation. Then, counting aloud in a voice like a grunt, he began to apply the cane to the pilgrim's back. Against his will, the pilgrim grunted, too, as the cane landed and then moaned and before the tenth was applied howled a little.

The soldiers released him from the cuffs and the sergeant handed him his robe. Gingerly the pilgrim adjusted it over his bleeding shoulders and stepped out into the street.

"Remember," the sergeant said. "No brawling."

The pilgrim thought he would remember.

The streets were dark. Curfew had rung while he had been in the captain's office, and the streets were deserted as well. The pilgrim shivered, and the involuntary movement made his back hurt anew. He had to get away quickly, he knew, but which way and where?

"Pilgrim," someone said. "Kelley!"

The pilgrim started and turned his whole body to face a particularly impenetrable area of darkness.

"It's me, Susannah." The girl came out of the darkness into the patch of light cast from the window above, where a candle flickered and the captain, no doubt, was working on his interminable reports which one day, he hoped, would get him to Court.

"You did take the identification," the pilgrim said.

"Yes, and then I had no way to get it back without telling you, and I didn't want to do that. Anyway, I thought a captain in the Emperor's secret police ought to have a taste of the Emperor's justice."

The pilgrim eased his shoulders into a more comfortable position. "I have," he said ruefully.

Susannah made a crooning sound and moved forward as if to remove his robe.

"Never mind. We've no time. In about fifteen minutes the captain is going to send his troops after me."

"But you've already been punished."

"He is going to reflect that I may be Captain Leonard Kelley after all. And he is going to consider that I will remember him when I get back to those who know me. And he will suspect that I will see he is taken care of in the nicest possible way. Rather than take that chance, he would rather kill me now."

"Follow me," Susannah said, and she led him through dark streets, between ruins, and up the beginning slope of a hill.

In the distance, as they climbed, were the sounds of a horse stomping and a cart rattling as it moved forward and back and a distant voice shouting imprecations. "He was not a very bright officer," the pilgrim said. "It was more like twenty-five minutes."

"There's a little village on the other side of this hill," Susannah said.

"That's the first place the soldiers would look for us."

"Of course. But right up on top of this hill, where according to legend there once was a university which was burned at the start of the Lowbrow Rebellion, is the villa of a witch-doctor."

"And you think he will take us in?"

"Why not?"

"The captain of Emperor Bartlett's secret police?"

"A pilgrim. We all have pasts."

"Not like mine. I've even burned witches."

"The witch-doctors always have known who you are and what you want, right from the first moment you started studying with the witch-doctor near Denver."

"And what did I want?"

"To find out as much as possible about the witch-doctors so the Emperor could use their powers to enlarge his empire."

The pilgrim made a sound of dismay or humor.

"True?" Susannah said.

"True enough," he admitted.

"And now?"

"I don't know," he said. "I've seen many ways of life, and there is much to be said for each of them."

"Anyway," Susannah said, "we're not going to the villa. He's gone."

"Where then?"

"To the chapel."

"Why?"

"Why else? To pray." And without further conversation she led the pilgrim up the hill to his salvation.

VII

The villa was identical with all the others, low, sprawling, lighted, potent. Behind it was the domed chapel, standing like a silo in the night.

Susannah led him to it, for the pilgrim had a strange reluctance to enter the building. She urged him through the doorway. There was nothing new about it. Both of them had entered similar chapels in other places at other times, separately. Susannah pressed a button that closed the door behind them.

"Well, they can't get at us; that's for sure," the pilgrim said. "But we can't get out either, and they're likely to post a guard out there until we get hungry enough to come out."

"I think the truth is here, somewhere, if we can only discover it," Susannah said.

She motioned him up a ladder to the meditation room. They sat in the two padded chairs and meditated.

"A pilgrim is a witch-doctor's way of making another witch-doctor," the pilgrim muttered.

"What did you say?"

The pilgrim repeated it. "Just something I thought of."

"What else did you think of?"

"Why are witch-doctors?"

"Yes," Susannah said. "Go on."

"What do they do besides serve others? Because they must do something. They do something human. Right?"

"Or witch-doctorish."

"That's the same thing, a kind of special humanness. And where do they do it? Everywhere that we have seen them they live alone. Perhaps somewhere else on this world they are all witch-doctors together, and they do something."

"Something wonderful."

"Or something terrible."

"Never."

"If we have seen all there is to see—there may be stranger ways of living, but we must think that what we have seen on our travels represents what is typical—then the witch-doctors must do what they do somewhere not on this world."

"Yes," Susannah said.

"Yes," the pilgrim said.

"We have found the truth."

"We have found the truth."

"They say," Susannah said, "that when a pilgrim has found the truth he should press the button in the meditation room of a chapel, and if he has truly found it he will ascend to heaven. And if he has not found it he will die."

"That is what they say."

"Shall I press it?"

"Press it!"

Susannah pressed the button in front of her. As she did so, a jolt rocked them back in their chairs. Metal straps closed around their arms and legs and waists and pulled them tightly into the chairs.

But they were pulled tighter still by some other force. It tugged at all the parts of their body, their cheeks, eyeballs, face, arms, legs, inner organs. . . . And it tugged and tugged for an eternity. Suddenly eternity was over, and they floated in their straps, sickeningly free of pressures but oppressed by a new sensation of falling.

Then the force tugged them back once more into the cushioned chairs for another eternity and released them once more and they floated again and they vomited. The vomit floated in globules in the air about them.

"Congratulations," said a voice without a body, a voice which sounded a little like the voice of their witch-doctor, whoever he might be, and a little like the voice of God. "You have found the truth, or by accident you have placed yourself in great jeopardy. The next few minutes and hours will determine whether you will find what you have been seeking or you will be dead."

The metal cuffs released them from their seats, and they, too, floated in the air. It was a bit like the gymnastic exercises he had performed in the witch-doctor's school.

"You now are in orbit around the earth, which means you are out in space where there is no air, nothing to breathe, no food, nothing to eat, and either no heat or too much heat, and you will freeze or burn.

"In the lockers around this room, which now are open, is equipment which you must use if you are to survive. If you have an unconquerable fear of machines or an unreasonable prejudice against them, you are doomed. Your life depends upon the proper use of these machines. You also must depend upon what my voice tells you, for you have only two other referents for this kind of environment: your schooling and your native and conditioned adaptability."

Susannah and the pilgrim were becoming a little better accustomed to the novel sensation of free fall. The globs of rejected food and fluids, however, were a nuisance as they brushed into them and the globs spread over their bodies. Susannah found an open container and lid in one of the lockers and chased the larger globs around the room until she had most of them captured. She discovered that if she kept the container in forward motion the contents would remain at the bottom but if she forgot they would float out again. The pilgrim found a cloth and swatted at the remainder until the air was reasonably clear. Then container and cloth were pushed into a receptacle marked "wastes."

When they finished they learned that they could maneuver themselves reasonably well in this new environment.

Meanwhile the voice continued with its instructions and admonitions. "Your capsule—this machine for traveling in space which encloses you—is approaching a space station, a village for living in space, where there is no air, no food, and too much or too little heat. You must not only survive the environment in this capsule, which will get deadlier, you must find a way to survive a passage through the hostile environment outside and make your way, with some novel method of travel, to the space station. Once you have accomplished this, your ordeal, your final examination, will be over.

"Everything you need is around you. Think, adapt, use. Remember that nothing is intrinsically evil or intrinsically good. Everything depends upon how it is used."

The pilgrim looked at Susannah; she was looking at him. They both looked around the room at the many lockers yet unopened which might hold the key to their survival. The pilgrim felt a flare of rebellion at the unfairness of this test, thrust upon them so unexpectedly, upon which depended their continued existence. They were not ready for this alien experience. And then he thought, and his resentment began to fade, how could they be ready for something as alien as this if they had not been born into it?

"You may be feeling that you have gambled your lives without foreknowledge of the game, that had you known the stakes you would not have played. But this is true of all men. No one ever knows the stakes except that at the end, however long delayed, there will be death.

"Our goal is to breed a new man who can adapt to the machine and the environment of machine-aided civilization. Some we can breed here in space, where man and child must learn to depend utterly on the machine to sustain life, for one mistake usually is fatal. Thus the natural law assumes new vitality: the survival of the fittest.

"Many others we recruit from earth, where the store of genetic material—of that which makes men and women have children like themselves—is still far greater than we can muster and still of infinite potential."

Susannah and the pilgrim began to work their way through the contents of the lockers. Enigmatic lessons that he had learned in the witch-doctor's school were returning to the pilgrim with new meaning.

"Here is food," Susannah said. "A kind of paste that you squirt into your mouth like this. And a kind of fluid that you suck through a tube. At least we won't starve, not immediately."

"And here are a couple of funny suits," the pilgrim said.

"They look like they're made of silver."

"But they're flexible, except for the joints and a crazy kind of helmet."

Susannah came over to look at them. "If there's no air outside, then we couldn't breathe. We would die if we didn't take air with us. Maybe this is meant to hold the air around us."

"That's it," the pilgrim said. "And maybe these tubes are meant to contain extra air so that you can take more air than what the suit would contain. Look! There's a place in the back where something like this can be attached." He fiddled with the closed tube and a gush of cold air came out. He sniffed. "Smells all right, but cold."

"I think we ought to put them on right now," said Susannah.

The voice continued to talk to them. "The breed of man as a whole was incapable of living with machines and with science because it took from them the power of decision over their own lives and deaths. They rebelled. Most of them died, unable to survive without the abundance created by the machine. Some, who had proved their ability to adapt to new conditions, went into space. They wanted to survive, of course, but also they wanted man to survive and his pursuit of knowledge to survive. They wanted him to learn more about himself, about his past, about his environment, about his future, about his place in the universe.

"And he is doing this—man, not superman. The traits were always there, the potential for creativity and adaptability and adventurousness, just as there was in man the content of the villager, the hunger of the Emperor, the lust of the mercenary, the greed of the shopkeeper, the inquisitiveness of the Neo-Scientist, the simplicity of the Luddite.

"Out of this mix of traits, we select intelligence and adaptability and benevolence by making them a matter of survival."

The pilgrim was helping Susannah into her silver suit. Getting into it would have been difficult enough under normal conditions, but in weightlessness it was nearly impossible.

"How do we survive?" the voice continued. "How do we get the wealth to mount our expeditions to the planets of this system? How do we maintain our villas on earth? It comes down to energy, which is a kind of wealth; indeed in the end it is the only real kind of wealth. And in space energy is free. There is too much of it, so much that it will kill you if you don't respect it. And we are, as well, the sole users of atomic power, the surprising energy of the very small. For materials we mine the moon and the inhospitable areas of earth and its seas. We are rich.

"But wealth, like anything else, is neither good nor evil. It must be used properly. On earth we use it to help, freely, without interfering in men's free choices. In space we use it to move onward and outward, as man must do to be man, respecting all life and particularly respecting all possible thinking life, although we have found none yet. This is what we live by."

By now Susannah was into her suit, and the pilgrim fastened a tube of air onto her back, turned the valve, and hoped it would work. Then he helped her put on the helmet and fasten it. She motioned frantically at his suit and then himself. He floated and inserted his legs into the silvery material.

"Within a few minutes deceleration—slowing down— and minor course adjustments will begin," the voice said, "and you must be back in your chairs or you will be rattled around in this capsule like dice in a box. You might be injured. If you have made good use of your time, you will be in the space suits by now. If you are not, there is no time to start and complete the job.

"Five minutes after deceleration, the capsule door will open and the air in the capsule will rush out. If you are not properly protected you will die within a minute or so. If you are protected you will see, outside the port, the space station known as 'Truth.' If you make it to that station and into it, you will be one of us."

The pilgrim had struggled his suit closed and was trying to work the helmet into position with his clumsy, gloved hands while Susannah fastened the tube to his back.

"Take your places in the chairs," said the voice. "Now! And good luck to you."

They moved quickly to the chairs. Once settled into the chairs by pulling themselves down by the arms, they found their arms and legs again encircled. Almost as soon as that happened, they were tugged deep into the cushions again and then tugged from one side to another. After a moment the shifting weights vanished, and they were free.

Susannah sprang back to his helmet, checked the catches to see if all were closed, and finding one open, closed it. Not unlike monkeys searching each other's fur for salt, he did the same for her.

In the midst of their inspections, a gust spun them around. The air leaving, the pilgrim thought. He caught Susannah and braced himself against one of the seats until the gusts subsided.

"Are you all right?" he asked.

Inside her helmet her eyes were looking at him. He saw her lips move.

"I can't hear you," he said.

She shook her head. He shrugged.

He motioned her toward the door and then halted beside a locker they had not yet opened. He opened it. Inside was a rope and a pair of small hand machines. He did not know what they were for, but he grabbed them and then preceded Susannah down the ladder.

At the outer door he looked out the opening from which the door was completely gone—and saw the stars. For a moment his senses rebelled and he felt that he might be sick again. But he recalled his schooling about the stars and took a deep breath and forced himself to stare back at the staring stars, set in the blackest night, where a man might fall for ever and ever, without end, into infinity and beyond. And he turned to Susannah, who was staring past his shoulder, and fastened the rope around both of them with clumsy gloves, and tried to tie a square knot that he hoped would hold.

He gave her one of the hand machines. When she looked at him questioningly he looked blank. Then he eased himself out of the doorway. He floated free, and then Susannah, too, was free, and they floated above the capsule and they saw the earth above them.

It hung there in the black sky, huge, with misty mountains and shrouded blue seas and brown and green patches of earth, all muted into pastels by a veil of air. And suddenly the earth flipped over and was beneath them. The pilgrim gasped and tried to claw for support, and there was none. He forced himself to look away.

He saw the sun, clear and burning, as he had never seen it before, and he looked away quickly lest he go blind.

He saw the space station, a large wheel turning in the black sky, surrounded by metal bubbles that floated freely around it. So close and yet so hopelessly far away.

Susannah had been inspecting the machine the pilgrim had given her. She closed her gloved hand on it, and it hissed. It emitted a white exhaust. Alarmed, she released her grasp on it, and it shot away before she could grab it again. It receded quickly and soon was lost in the distance.

Susannah tapped the pilgrim's helmet and pointed at the machine in his hand and at the one that had disappeared toward the overhanging-undergirding earth, pointed at the direction it had been pointed and then indicated that the pilgrim should point his machine in a direction opposite the space station and squeeze its handle.

The pilgrim had seen and understood. Lessons he had learned about physics and chemistry and astronomy were coming back to him in a flood. There was something about an action and an equal and opposite reaction.

He pointed the machine and squeezed and released. He looked over his shoulder. The space station was closer. He squeezed again. The two space-suited figures accelerated toward the station.

But they missed the station by fifty feet. Quickly the pilgrim turned and fired in the opposite direction, but the maneuver took time and some of the precious contents of the hand machine to stop their progress and then reverse it. But the space station stopped receding and began to come back toward them once more.

At that point the little machine gave its last little puff. The pilgrim drew back his arm to throw it away and changed his mind. He checked their progress and direction and then, as he saw they might miss again, he carefully threw the machine in a direction calculated to send them closer.

As the space station grew closer, the pilgrim fumbled with the rope that bound him to Susannah. He loosened the knot and forced one end of the rope into Susannah's hand and held the other firmly in his. He placed his foot against Susannah's side and spun her away from him in the direction of the space station.

As they approached the station, they would have passed through the gap between the rim of the wheel and the hub, but the rope held between them caught the spoke and spun them around the spoke until they clanged against it and hung on grimly.

There were handholds on the spoke. After the pilgrim had regained his breath and his nerve, he began pulling himself with painful care toward the hub, holding the end of the rope in one hand so that Susannah would not slip away. It seemed to him that they crawled forever before they reached the hub.

The pilgrim searched for an entrance. He found a crack. He traced it. Beside the crack was a handle. He pulled it. The door swung open. Working carefully so that they did not lose their grasp on the hub at any time, the pilgrim and Susannah made their way through the door and into a small, tubular room. Opposite the door they had entered was another door and another handle. The pilgrim pulled it. The door behind them closed. A light above them and one below them came on.

The pilgrim felt as if he were a puddle of boneless flesh within his suit. Through Susannah's helmet he could see that she, too, was breathing deeply.

After a minute or two the door in front of them swung back. Gloved men moved surely to help them through the doorway. They seemed like ordinary men in coveralls. Well, the pilgrim thought, perhaps not quite like ordinary men. There was a certain calm sureness about them, in the way they moved in this weightless condition, a serenity of features, an air of infinite capacity. They moved quickly to take the helmets from the pilgrim's head and then Susannah's. They began stripping away the silver suits.

As the last part of their suits was removed, an older man came forward. He floated through the air as if it were the most natural method of locomotion imaginable. He held out his hands to both of them.

"Welcome!" he said in a tone that made them sure they were indeed welcome, that he was glad they had made it. "My name is John Wilson. That won't mean anything to you. But welcome. Welcome to the company of witches."